SHADOW OF A MAN

By: Harold P. Voyles

A play about Appalachia

DEDICATION

This book is dedicated to my wife, Merida, whose faith and wisdom made writing *"Shadow of a Man"* possible.

SHADOW OF A MAN

As the partridge sitteth on eggs and hatcheth them not, so he that getteth riches and not by right shall leave them in the midst of his days and at his end shall be a fool. *Jeremiah 17:11*

PREFACE

"Why do you write about Appalachia?" a friend once asked me. Somehow reminiscing about my youth in Harlan County, KY, has given me a greater appreciation for the land and the people.

Although I have not lived in the bluegrass state for 28 years, I still call Kentucky home. I was raised at Lynch, once one of the largest coal mining camps in America, boasting a population of 11,000 after World War II. Today the population is about 1,000.

By most estimates, Appalachia had the largest out-migration in U.S. history, with over one million people leaving the region to seek a better life elsewhere.

Over the years, many have sought to paint a realistic portrait of Appalachia through music, movies, documentaries, television and literature. Unfortunately, not all have done so with insight, understanding and an appreciation of the culture.

Someone once said, "You can't explain Appalachia. You just have to live it." In my play, *Shadow of a Man*, I attempt to explain a small part of the story. It is for you, dear reader, to decide if I have done it well.

Harold P. Voyles

SHADOW OF A MAN

The time is 1960 in Hoedown, a fictional mining town in Harlan County, KY. Numerous mine closings during the past decade have devastated the county.

However, people are encouraged when a large coal company announces plans to greatly expand mining operations and provide jobs for the idle miners. To do so the company needs additional acreage for their proposed expansion.

Will Poser, head of his family, is the largest landowner with 25 acres that the company covets because of its prime location. Will, who keeps negotiations with the company a secret, faces the difficult decision of continuing a way of life that has survived for generations, or selling the land for more money than the family could imagine.

Jesse Collins, former coal miner turned preacher, faces his own struggles. Jesse's life is intertwined with the Poser family as he attempts to maintain a friendship of more than two decades with Thalia Poser, Will's wife. However, Jesse's commitment to his faith as he confronts hypocrisy and greed is a heavy burden to bear.

The play attempts to provide diverse points of view suggesting there are no easy answers to difficult problems-not in America-and especially not in Appalachia.

CAST LISTING

1. Hawthorne Cartwright
2. Jesse Collins
3. Clive McAlister
4. Thurman Moberly
5. Hankins Poser
6. Ollie Poser
7. Thalia Poser
8. Will Poser
9. Harley Simpkins
10. Chester Wiggins
11. Blake Whitaker

CHARACTERS

Hawthorne Cartwright (deacon chairman)
Hawthorne is a manipulative, pompous, yet harmless and somehow likeable rascal. For example, Hawthorne stands to profit personally if he can persuade the pastor to encourage church members to sell their land and church property to the coal company.

Jesse Collins (preacher)
A coal miner turned preacher, Jesse, in younger days, was the fiancé of Thalia Poser. Jesse now carries the duel burden of pastoring his flock and still yearning for his lost love. Jesse is a man who gives so much he is almost running on empty as he tries to save the people and himself.

Clive McAlister (mine superintendent)
Clive wants to expand mining operations, but to do so his company needs land owned by the mountain families. Because of its prime location, obtaining the Poser property is vital to the proposed expansion. Clive, whose loyalty is primarily to the company, knows he must win the trust of the miners if he is to succeed.

Thurman Moberly (chief detective)
Thurman, head of the company's police force, is a veteran of mine battles fought over the years. Although Thurman is hard-nosed, he respects the miners and wants to treat them fairly. He yearns for a more peaceful life, but realizes he must do his duty if he is to hang on until retirement.

Thalia Poser (Will Poser's wife)
Thalia prepares for changes in her life as her husband ponders selling land owned by their family for decades. Thalia dreams of becoming an artist as she struggles to maintain her friendship with Jesse without being disloyal to her preoccupied and often insensitive husband.

Hankins Poser (Will's father)
Hankins, a widower and retired miner, often reminisces about the past, particularly Sarah, his beloved wife. Hankins dreams of moving back to the camp house where he raised his family decades earlier. Driven by a need he does not quite understand, Hankins feels the move will complete something he has left undone.

Ollie Poser (son)
Ollie, a throwback to an earlier generation, believes he can harvest timber, farm the land, and thus remain free of the coal industry's influence. Ollie loves the land and vows to keep it in the family. This pits him against Will, his father, who believes the old way of life is gone forever.

Will Poser (husband and father)
Will worked in the mines while living on the family's 25 acres, a mile from town. For two decades, he farmed the land by day and mined coal at night. A self-proclaimed old man at 40, Will plans to sell property to the company and buy a place in town, likely alienating everyone in his family.

Harley Simpkins (head company engineer)
Harley basks in his recent accomplishment of building a dam at the head of Flatgap Hollow. He understands that a safe, secure dam is vital to the company's financial well-being. However, possible violence makes the dam a likely target for those opposing the company.

Chester Wiggins (Hankins's friend)
Chester who believes "coal mining gets in your blood" had left the coalfields repeatedly, but always returned when the mine reopened. Chester and Hankins's friendship is rock solid, forged from shared experiences of poverty, brute labor, and union organizing.

Blake Whittaker (company detective)
Blake longs to escape the coalfields and seek another way of life. He resents the miners and believes they deserve their lot in life. Blake's duties often pit him against the miners, but he lacks the wisdom to relate to a people he does not care to understand.

SHADOW OF A MAN
A Three-Act Play

Act One
Scene One: The Cabin in the Hollow
Scene Two: Jesse and Thalia
Scene Three: Ollie and Hankins
Scene Four: The negotiations
Scene Five: Suppertime at the Cabin

Act Two
Scene One: Will and Ollie
Scene Two: Gap Hollow Baptist Church
Scene Three: Dawn at the Cabin
Scene Four: The second Meeting
Scene Five: The family Circle

Act Three
Scene One: The Truth Shall Set You Free
Scene Two: The Last Meeting
Scene Three: You Can Go Home Again
Scene Four: The Dam
Scene Five: The Healing Has Begun

Epilogue

ABOUT THE AUTHOR

Harold P. Voyles worked as an underground miner in Harlan and Pike Counties in the 70's and early 80's. In 2000, he published a book of prose titled *Appalachian Sketches*, which depicts life in a mining camp. Currently, Voyles resides with Merida, his wife, in Fernandina Beach, Florida.

Shadow of A Man is a work of fiction. Although the setting is Harlan County, KY and the towns of Harlan, Cumberland and Hazard are real, other places are purely fictional. In addition, names, characters and incidents are a product of the author's imagination and any resemblance to actual persons or events is coincidental.

Shadow of a Man
By: Harold P. Voyles

Act One
Scene One

Lights rise in the cabin in a hollow near Hoedown, a mining town in eastern Kentucky. A mandolin plays softly in the background. The cabin's kitchen is sparse containing a kitchen table with four chairs, a rectangular table and an old-fashioned cooking stove and a closet. The room has one small window (stage left) a front door (stage right) and back door (center stage).

Will Poser sits at the table clasping his half-full coffee mug. Will, 46, is tall, lanky and ruggedly handsome, but a smirk marks him for an unpleasant companion. Will often broods, suggesting there is a lingering hurt that he is reluctant to confront.

Thalia, his wife, a youthful 43, is tomboyish but pretty. A life of labor gives her physical strength that perplexes Will. Thalia is witty, yet crestfallen. Discontent swirls about her while she yearns for something she cannot articulate, making her seem aloof to those who care for her.

Meanwhile, Thalia hums softly as she flattens dough with a rolling pin at the rectangular table near the window. She works with the dexterity of someone who performs a task so often it becomes effortless.

Unease permeates the air, but it is difficult to pinpoint the source. Through the kitchen window, daylight peeps around the clouds making shadows prance about the room hinting of an intruder. Silence is broken when Will coughs and begins to speak.

Will: You've been humming that dang song all morning. Why can't you just go ahead and sing it? It's getting on my nerves.

Thalia: I'll sing when I get through humming.

Will: I've been trying all morning to get that tune out of my head. It's about to drive me crazy.

Thalia: It's a short trip for some folks.

Will: What's that supposed to mean?

Thalia does not reply as she cuts dough in strips and places layers over a deep dish filled with apples. She looks out the window at the hill below and absent-mindedly runs a hand through her hair to pat back a loose strand. She opens the oven door and places the dish inside the wood-burning stove before slamming the door and quickly jerking her hand away. She again looks out the window. Gradually a smile blankets her face. Will stands suddenly and clears his throat.

Will: If we ever get a big coal company in here, in a year or two, we'll have electricity in Fancy Hollow. No more kerosene lamps or candles. Maybe we can get an oil furnace so we don't burn coal. I get tired of soot everywhere.

Thalia: You can't beat coal for heat and I like burning candles.

Will: Fancy Hollow. Lord, what a name for this place. Ain't nothing fancy about it at all.

Thalia: Compared to the way folks live in the mining camp, I'd say we're doing fine. You know how Fancy Hollow got its name don't you?

Will: Uh, I don't recall.

Thalia: Daddy named it after his first sweetheart. Fancy died when she was only 16. You remember the year the flu killed about five or six people in Hoedown.

Will: Yeah, Lambert, my first cousin, was just a baby when he got sick and died in three days. Was it 31' or 32'? Seems like I can't remember anything anymore unless it's useless information.

Thalia: I'm not sure, but I remember after Momma died, Daddy told me he loved only two women his whole life. Fancy and Momma. That's how Fancy Hollow got its name. I can't believe I don't remember her last name.

Will: Daddy? Lord, Thalia, you're what, 42, 43, and still call him daddy. He's been gone nine years now.

Thalia: What can I say? I was a daddy's girl. Daddy and Momma raised four boys and one girl and they determined to make me a tom-boy. Daddy said if I'd been a boy, I could've whipped George and Troy. They were the oldest. I could hold my own with the youngest two and I could whip Milton until he turned fourteen.

Will: I swear your family would rather fight than eat steak. Even your dog and cat was mean. George and Troy were bullies. If they worked at a job like they did fighting, they'd had more money than a bluegrass lawyer. But the two youngest, Milton and Truman, I liked a little bit.

Thalia: My brothers were good boys at heart. But Lord, they loved to play pranks. I remember one Halloween night they ran through the coal camp and toppled 14 outhouses. They claimed it was a record.

Will: Your family don't have much to brag about, do they?

Thalia: They were always getting in a ruckus, but we were a loving family. Daddy would sit me on his knee and ask me if I was his little girl. If I'd say no, he'd tickle me and sometimes I'd wet my pants. Momma would get mad and say, 'Lord Ah mighty Daddy.'

Will: Spoiled you bad. Whole family thought you could do no wrong. I recall I made you cry that time when we broke up for a week. Truman and George caught me at the company store and said if I made you cry again I'd better light out for Detroit.

Thalia: Four boys and one girl. What would you expect?

Will: Sound like a little girl still calling him daddy.

Thalia: I just never got used to calling him father, or dad. A daddy is different.

Will: Just a different name for the same thing.

Thalia: It's more than that. A daddy is a father who isn't afraid to love.

Will: I know what you're getting at. You're always speaking in double meanings.

Thalia: The pie will be done soon. Don't you love the smell of apples and cinnamon? I really love a wood-burning fire in the fall to beat back the chill. Seems like the cold eventually beats down the good things. If we get electricity in Fancy Hollow, things will change. All the changes won't be good.

Will: I swear Thalia, the harder I try to make conversation the less sense you make. You shouldn't spend so much time painting. It causes you to drift off into another world. Sometimes, I feel like I don't even know you.

Thalia: Maybe you never did.

Will: I ain't going to argue all day. That's all we do anymore. Where the devil is that mailman anyway? Postal Service should've fired Doak Owens years ago. They suspended him twice and it made him even slower. He'd stop and chat with a tree stump.

Thalia: You can get more sense out a tree stump than some people.

Will: There you go again. I swear Thalia, sometimes talking to you is like talking to the mule.

Thalia: I just hope you don't argue with the mule with the same enthusiasm as you do me.

Will, now angry and scowling, walks the length of the cabin twice before he pitches his coffee out the back door and slams the mug on the table.

Will: I'm going to the post office. If Doak comes by, put the letter up. I don't want you or Ollie reading it before I do.

When Will opens the door to leave, Thalia begins to sing loudly and slightly off key. Will hunches his shoulders and lowers his head as the lyrics bullies him off the porch and down the path to his truck. (Lights fade.)

> *Whenever I hear church bells ring*
> *My spirit soars and I joyfully sing.*

Scene Two

When lights rise in the cabin, it is past noon. Thalia sits at the kitchen table with a coffee mug and a large art book. An assortment of artist's brushes, paints and pens lie next to a sketching pad. She stares intently at a drawing and is startled when a heavy, strong hand raps

16

the door. She shakes the table spilling paint on her paper. Thalia mutters under her breath, and then yells for the visitor to enter.

A short, stocky man, about Thalia's age and height, steps through the door swiping at his coat. Pastor Jesse Collins smiles broadly, but moves cautiously as if each step has been pre-determined. His eyes shine with a light whose source is not easily discernible. When Thalia sees Jesse, she throws her shoulders back, lifts her head and smiles.

Thalia: Pastor, if it's not too much trouble, would you mind shutting the door?

Jesse: Glad to, Mrs. Poser.

Thalia: Jesse, what are you up to besides pestering the devil?

Jesse: Just got back from a revival. You remember when we were courting and went to a revival over in Harlan. That preacher was a snake-handler.

Thalia: I've forgotten a lot over the years, but not that.

Jesse: We joked that if I became a preacher I wouldn't handle poisonous snakes. But who'd thought I'd actually become a man of the word.

Thalia: Not me, for sure.

Jesse: I can't believe it's spitting snow the first day of November.

Thalia: It's the second. The second day of November. It's a wonder you know when to show up for church.

Jesse: I did forget a Wednesday night service my first year preaching and Deacon Cartwright wanted to run me off.

Thalia: You should've let him. You'd had a lot less worries if you'd stayed in the mines. You almost spilt the church that time you shoved him up against a wall. Did they teach you that in seminary?

Jesse: Not unless you take a loose interpretation of The Good Lord works in mysterious ways. Truth is Hawthorne never did like me.

Thalia: Well, I wonder why?

Jesse: As I recall, neither did your dad. He said I was too ornery to be a man of God and wouldn't last a year. So Deacon Cartwright wasn't the only one who wanted to run me off.

Thalia: Daddy wanted to see if you'd fight for what was yours. But you cut tail and run like a third-grader getting clear of a playground bully.

Jesse: You were never mine, Mrs. Poser.

Thalia: I have a first name and you should know it by now.

Jesse: Mrs. Uh, I mean Thalia.

Thalia: You know, Jesse, after all these years, I never once asked you why you left. Well, I'm asking you now. Why didn't you stay and fight?

Jesse: Thalia, those five acres I was going to buy for us, sold out from under me. Old man Spencer said he'd give me four months to get up the money. I worked in that foundry in Cleveland until I thought I'd died and gone to the lake of fire. Now when I preach about hell, that foundry always crosses my mind. Seems like something always comes to mind that means something else.

Thalia: There was other land.

Jesse: Came home with my left pocket so full of money I leaned to one side. But Spencer had already sold the property to the Johnson boys. The night I found out, if I hadn't got drunk and got my truck stuck in a ditch, I'd shot Spencer for sure.

Thalia: You men! Why did the good Lord make so many of you? Is land worth more than everything else? How can things that should mean so little mean so much? You left without saying goodbye and stayed gone three years. We thought you were dead.

Jesse: In a way, I was dead.

Thalia: That can't be the real reason you left. There's got to be something else.

Jesse: There is something else and one day I just might tell you.

Thalia: You never told me where you went either. I can't believe I've waited over 20 years to ask you. Doak Owens said you were in California.

Jesse: Doak's got a tongue like an insulted mother-in-law. First word comes to mind, he'll let fly.

Thalia: Well, where did you go? Or are you too ashamed to tell?

Jesse: Not much to tell. I went back to Cleveland, then Detroit and ended up in Chicago. I lived there for 14 months and made good money. But I stayed holed up in my room on the fourth floor and hardly got out. If I'd stayed much longer, I'd probably never left that room.

Thalia: Jesse, I don't understand. You were always the life of the party. What happened?

Jesse: Sometimes things move so slow you don't realize it until it's too late. It's like wearing out a good pair of boots. You're half-barefooted before you notice they're giving out.

And when you lose something and got no chance of getting it back, it's like it never was. I remember one summer us kids dammed up the creek with logs and boulders. We had us a fine pool of water about four feet deep. To us it was a river. But one day the company guards caught us swimming and made us tear out the dam. In a few minutes, the water was only shin-deep. A week later, it seemed like us kids had never been swimming in our lives. That's how the past seemed to me. Like it never was.

Thalia: Jesse, didn't you have friends?

Jesse: I made plenty of friends in Cleveland and Detroit. I courted a lot of pretty girls too. Those girls, especially in Detroit, loved to hear me talk. They'd tease me about my hillbilly accent. But when I got to Chicago, I just couldn't do it anymore. I'd stay home on Saturday night and prop my feet on the window sill and watch the pavement cool off. It was so hot it felt like the streets hated you and wanted you to die. When fall came, I'd sit by my window for hours and swear I could smell wood fires burning. I missed October in the mountains so bad I could barely stand it.

Thalia: You always went to church before. Why didn't you go to church in Chicago?

Jesse: I'm not sure. I'd go out Sunday evening, sit on a church's steps and listen to the singing and preaching. But I never felt like I belonged anywhere. I couldn't figure why what use to give me joy caused me pain. If Mom hadn't died, I guess I'd still be in Chicago looking out that window.

Thalia: Lord, Jesse.

Jesse: I need to go. I thought Will was here and there's something I wanted to ask him. He's got a good head for business.

Thalia: You're the pastor out visiting his flock. There's nothing wrong with that.

Jesse: You haven't been to church in eight months.

Thalia: You remember that when you couldn't remember to take your hat the last time you visited.

Jesse: How come you remember the hat?

Thalia: The last time I went to church, you kept losing your train of thought. Cartwright told the other deacons he didn't get a thing out of the sermon. I thought I was doing you a favor by staying away.

Jesse: You sat in the first row. You could have sat farther back.

Thalia: By the back door so I could be the first to leave?

Jesse: I need to go.

Thalia: Stay. I fixed a fresh pot of coffee and the apple pie is ready.

Jesse: I love the smell of apple pie baking. I love the fall but I get the blues when the last leaf falls. Say, are you painting again? You could paint scenery for the Christmas play next month.

When Jesse finishes his pie and coffee, he scoots his chair close to Thalia and sees that she is sketching him. He starts to touch her left cheek with the back of his hand but a cloud passes the window again finally freeing the sun. When he sees his shadow upon the wall-a twisted, grotesque replica of himself, he jerks his hand away. Thalia folds the sketch of Jesse twice and hands it to him. He puts it in his shirt pocket and pats his heart. She smiles.

Thalia: Jesse, Jesse. Always so strong.

Jesse: If you only knew.

Thalia: Don't you get lonely? Don't you have somebody?

Jesse: It's been two years, but its worse at Christmas. You'd think I'd overcome it being a preacher. Fact is I'm no different from Will or anybody else. When you're alone too long, you start dying a little at a time. The problem is everybody knows it but you.

Thalia: You're nothing like Will.

Jesse: I can't care for a family on my salary.

Thalia: Never say you're like Will again.

Jesse: I seem to make the wrong move every time. If it was raining ham sandwiches, I'd be inside taking a nap. I'll think about a thing until I can't think no more. But when it's time for action, I go left when I should go right. Sometimes I feel like there's two of me. I swear when I'm standing still, I think I see my shadow move like it's got a will of its own. And I don't even drink. Not anymore anyways.

Thalia: Nothing like him at all.

Jesse: Thalia, I have to go now.

Thalia: Come again and stay for supper.

Jesse: You know I like fried chicken.

Thalia: I wouldn't trust a preacher that didn't eat fried chicken.

Jesse: Thalia, you're something else.

Thalia: Jesse, I'm worried about you. I've never seen you talk so much. You're like a geyser. Usually I have to pull the words out of you.

Jesse: Oh, I'm doing fine. It's just…

Thalia: What Jesse? Tell me.

Jesse: Kind of hard to explain. I feel like I'm being pulled toward something I can't resist. I don't understand anything anymore. Did you know one time I was almost electrocuted in the mines?

Thalia: Lord, no.

Jesse: One day I walked past the transformer where a 7,200-volt supply cable was connected to the back. There must have been a small cut in the cable. You know I'm pretty stout, but it took all my strength to pull away from that cable. I was so weak when I sat down my hands shook. Somebody handed me a cup of coffee and I couldn't hold it still. A few minutes later, that cable blew. You wouldn't believe the noise. The electrician said I was lucky to be alive

Thalia: The Good Lord was looking out for you.

Jesse: It's weird, but a part of me wanted to give in to the pull. That's the way I feel now. I'm being drawn toward something that I fear yet yearn for. It's like there's something I'm meant to do and time is getting close.

Thalia: I heard you've been preaching on Revelations for three months now. You're happier when you preach about Jesus. I can see it in your face. Jesse, I'm afraid for you.

Suddenly Thalia clasps Jesse's hand and holds it against her cheek. Thalia's strength surprises Jesse when he tries to pull his hand away.

Jesse: Thalia, please.

Thalia: Jesse, Jesse, Jesse.

Jesse: I'm going now. Right now.

Thalia releases Jesse's hand and they both bow their heads. (Lights fade)

Scene Three

It is early evening when the lights rise in the cabin. The front door opens and Ollie stomps his feet on a rug by the door. The tall, lankly youth has a smile etched so deeply on his face it appears permanent. Ollie displays the joyful swagger of youth that is often imitated unconvincingly by adults. Ollie sniffs the air and smiles, because there are four dishes of food warming on the stove.

Hankins Poser, Ollie's granddad, steps through the bedroom door, (center stage) wearing overalls latched on one side. He has the physique of a much younger man, but his face belongs to someone receiving a social security check. Hankins moves with an energetic stoop as his twinkling eyes reveal a penchant for mischief and merriment in equal doses. When Hankins scratches himself, Ollie roars with laughter. Both sit down at the kitchen table.

Ollie: I could smell cornbread when I got on the front porch. Say, where's everybody? Where's Mom and Dad?

Hankins: They went to town for something, but I ain't sure when they'll be back. Your dad don't volunteer nothing, and I know better than to ask.

Ollie: They went to town together? Mom hates getting out when it turns cold. It sure is cold the first week of November.

Hankins: I remember when I was in fourth grade or was it fifth? Anyway, it snowed so deep one November I stayed in the house for three days. We cleared a path to the barn and outhouse and that was it. Mom had to switch me and Coy, my brother, every day for fighting. I guess we got on each other's nerves.

Ollie: Granddad, how come it snowed more, rained more and got hotter when you were a boy?

Hankins: Seemed that way to me. I swear I'm itching to death. Reckon your mom changed brands of washing powders. Ones that smell the best itches me the most.

Ollie: Granddad, you're getting old.

Hankins: Been old a long time. I remember my Momma, God rest her soul, saying she was tired of being tired. Didn't know what she meant then. I do now.

Ollie: Is your arthritis acting up again?

Hankins: They say the hot weather in Florida is good for aching joints.

Ollie: Why don't you go and find out?"

Hankins: Years ago, two friends and me talked about buying a boat and shrimping the waters down in Florida. But I'd never been happy leaving the mountains.

Ollie: You went up north a couple of times.

Hankins: I'd leave home looking for work and swear I wasn't ever coming back. Be doing fine. But when a new mine opened, in a month or two, I'd trudge home with my tail tucked between my legs. After a month, it seemed like I'd never been away.

Ollie: Dad wants me to leave and go to vocational school and learn welding. He's says it's good wages for the work. But Mom wants me to enroll in that two-year college over in Cumberland.

Hankins: I heard something about that.

Ollie: It opened last year. I reckon it's part of the University of Kentucky down in Lexington. I went to Lexington once to a horse race. Too many people, too much flatland, not enough hills.

Hankins: What about the army? Might do you some good. Lot of mountain boys join the service.

Ollie: Idea comes into Dad's head he can't get it out of there. If he mentions welding one more time, I'll, I swear I'll get me a bottle of moonshine from the Johnson boys. They make the best.

Hankins: Need to leave that stuff alone. Ain't nothing but a first cousin to kerosene.

Ollie: Dad said you drank more than your share over the years.

Hankins: Just when I had a cold, or to ease the pain in my joints.

Ollie: Your joints must have hurt an awful lot. But Granddad, listen. I can farm this place if Dad would let me clear a few more acres. There ain't nothing like growing something from God's green earth. When the plants peek out of the ground in the spring, I can almost see the Good Lord looking down and smiling.

Hankins: A man's love for the land runs deep. But a lot of families are giving up and selling out to the coal company. The McKnights, the Atkins, the Hatfields.

Ollie: The Hatfields? I don't believe it.

Hankins: That's what Doak Owens said.

Ollie: We'll never sell this land. We can't sell because the family cemetery is on the hill. Little Corey's buried there. He's the only brother I'll ever have. You know he died when he was only a month old.

Hankins: It's not right for a baby to die. It gets the whole world out of balance. Did you know Corey was supposed to be named Coy after my brother, but Doc Blevins was hard of hearing. He had poor eyesight too. Come to think of it, he wasn't much of a doctor.

Ollie: I heard Mom say something about it. But you don't think Dad would sell for any amount of money?

Hankins: Will wants to know the value of the land. He has to know what everything costs. If somebody buys a ten-year old washing machine, he'll ask the price.

Ollie: I won't let him sell the land.

Hankins: Maybe he won't sell.

Ollie: I'll stop him somehow. The other day, he let it slip about getting the land surveyed. I was so mad I stomped out of the house and spent the night in the woods.

Hankins: It's a wonder you don't get carried off by a black bear.

Ollie: I ain't seen a bear around here in years. Strip-mining has run them off.

Hankins: Well, anyway, your dad wanted the survey done to find out where the boundaries are. If you ain't careful, a coal company can end up with land that's been in the family 50 years. It might be yours, but if they say it's theirs, it'll end up theirs.

Ollie: That was in the old days.

Hankins: Still is the old days. You make trouble for a coal company and you'll find out quick enough. You remember Willie Williams? Why would a mother give a child one name for a first and last name? It wasn't like they'd run out of good names. He never was right in the head. Probably the reason.

Ollie: Went to court didn't he?

Hankins: Hee, hee. Willie thought he'd be smart and get him a lawyer over in Harlan. Turns out his lawyer was kin to the other side's lawyer. The judge was part - owner of a coalmine too. Poor Willie had a better chance of marrying the governor's daughter than he did of winning that lawsuit.

Ollie: I ain't afraid of no coal company. I whipped the mine superintendent's oldest boy last month and he never did a thing about it. He's two years older and ten pounds heavier, and I still gave him a good thumping.

Hankins: Doak Owens said he was bragging to some girls at church about giving you a shiner. I could see your black eye when I came out of the outhouse and you sitting on the front porch. I reckon he said the next time he'd black both of your eyes. Hee, hee.

Ollie: We'll see. I'll catch him in the pool hall sooner or later.

Hankins: Hee, hee, hee. (Lights fade)

Scene Four

Lights rise in Superintendent Clive McAlister's mine office, located in Hoedown. The office contains a desk and two chairs (center stage) and a door (stage right). Clive's office sits atop a hill overlooking the town, along with the post office, company store, warehouse and firehouse.

From the hilltop, the mining camp appears picturesque, but up close, the flaws are pronounced. The town has a beaten down look that rubs off on its citizens.

Below, on Main Street, are two restaurants with almost identical menus, two bars with the same jukebox tunes and brands of beer, a gas station, theatre, pool hall, six churches and a funeral parlor.

This morning Will waits to meet with McAlister. Will keeps removing a letter from his back pocket and reading it, perhaps hoping to find some overlooked detail. Will believes he is shrewd, but reminds himself that his grandfather lost his land and died penniless.

McAlister appears after 30 minutes. He is 50, stout, and possesses a thick head of salt and pepper hair that almost gives him a distinguished look. He reeks with the calm assurance of someone who was once poor, but now believes it can never happen to him again.

Clive: Will, sorry to keep you waiting.

Will: Been waiting all my life for somebody or something. So what's up?

Clive: The main office in Pittsburg had me on the phone all morning. I can't get any work done for spending hours on the darn phone.

Will: Your secretary said you wanted to see me right away.

Clive: Yes, of course. Will, this is the third time we've met to talk about purchasing your land. Headquarters is getting impatient. I'll need an answer before long.

Will: I've been thinking about this a lot. It's not an easy decision to make. Lately, it's kept me awake at night.

Clive: I sympathize with your position, but the company needs an agreement soon. We both know your land is the best location for a new coal preparation plant. We want the land, but not at any price. I can only go so far. I have people I have to answer to.

Will: I guess we'd all be happy if we didn't have to try to make other people happy. But you're already the largest landowner in the county.

Clive: True, but it would shorten our haulage if we had your twenty-some acres.

Will: Twenty-some? Its 25 acres.

Clive: The survey said 22 acres.

Will: It's been 25 acres for almost 40 years. It ain't shrunk none.

Clive: Well, we have to honor the surveyor's findings.

Will: Not me.

Clive: Look, Will, I've been more than patient with you. The deadline is drawing near for you to decide. You know enough about coalmining to understand we need a better haulage route.

Will: Like you always say, time is money.

Clive: The shorter the haulage, the less expense for the mine. When the company makes more profits, the miners earn better wages.

Will: I've heard that's the way it's supposed to work. Haven't seen it yet.

Clive: We've got a good coal preparation plant in Fire Creek. It needs some work, but its six miles to haul the coal by rail from there. If we get your land, we can build a bigger, cleaner and faster plant in Flatgap Hollow. It'll be the same seam of coal. We'll just mine from the north side instead of south.

Will: I see. You've got all the conveyor belts and railroad tracks anyway. Just reverse the belts and you're in business. So that's why you're building that dam at the mouth of the hollow.

Clive: The best thing to happen to this end of the county. No reason for Harlan to always get the best of everything. Now our young people won't have to leave the mountains to look for work. The state deciding to put the community college in our neck of the woods has changed everything.

Will: You're asking a lot. My wife inherited half the land from her old man. By rights, it's still hers.

Clive: In five years, we could have a new high school, new houses, nice restaurants and maybe even a Holiday Inn. But it all starts here.

Will: We've been lied to before.

Clive: Haven't I always been straight with you?

Will: It's according to what you mean by straight. If nobody agrees on what a crooked line is, it's hard for a straight line to claim it's straight.

Clive: How's this for straight? Five hundred jobs.

Will: What?

Clive: Five hundred jobs and that's just the beginning. Last year, I thought this guy Kennedy running for president was a joke. I said this country will never elect a Catholic. I figured since I'm Catholic I should know. But he's been all over West Virginia campaigning. I'm telling you he's going to win.

Will: You really think he can win?

Clive: I've never been so sure of anything in my life. For some reason, he's able to inspire people. He has a way of making people feel better about themselves. Never thought I'd say that about a Democrat.

Will: I don't have much faith in any of them.

Clive: This country has been in a slump, especially the coal market. Half the coal companies in eastern Kentucky have closed or gone broke this past decade. But Detroit is selling cars again. The steel mills are hiring. Coal-fired power plants are being built again. There's going to be a boom.

Will: You make it sound so easy.

Clive: It won't be easy. Making this thing work may be harder than anything I've done in a while. But the time is right. It's now or never.

Will: I want to believe you. God, I wish I could trust a coal company. It'd be the first time.

Clive: I don't deny we've made mistakes-some awful mistakes. But we can't keep fighting the battles our grandfathers and fathers fought or we'll both lose. We could lose out to oil. We're starting to import more oil from the Middle East. Mark my words, this thing could backfire on us one day. Let's keep the money and jobs in this country is what I say.

Will: I'll have to sleep on it. Last time I made a rash decision, I ended up married.

Clive: Ha, ha, yeah well. I've saved the best for last.

Will: Don't know if I can handle anymore good news. I might start expecting it.

Clive: In five years, we plan to employ 1,000 miners. What do you think about that?

Will: Please tell me you're exaggerating. Where would the people live? There's not enough houses left for 300 miners. The company tore down a fourth of the camp houses in the past five years.

Clive: Kennedy, JFK, whatever they call him, has been blasting coal companies for having mining camps. Headquarters wants to change our image and break with the past. Now get this. I was on the phone with headquarters before you got here. They want to start selling the camp houses to the miners.

Will: After all these years?

Clive: The newspapers, television and magazines all over the country hits us over this head with this thing every day. When you say the words coal camp, it leaves a bad taste in people's mouth. A miner will be able to buy his house for $200 a room. Just think of that.

Will: A drunk can knock the windows out of his house and not get arrested by the company police?

Clive: Once the house is yours, you can remodel it or paint it any color you want. Do whatever you want.

Will: Maybe some bright colors for this God-forsaken mining camp would help. No wonder it's so dreary, especially in winter, with all the drab colors.

Clive: Like I said, any color you want, or brick. They're even making this stuff called aluminum siding to put on houses.

Will: Siding made out of aluminum? It'll never catch on. Of course, management doesn't have to worry about those things. Most of you live in limestone houses that you own.

Clive: Now that you've assigned blame to the coal companies for all the country's problems, can we deal with the issue at hand. I know the perception is of a coal company abusing the workers. Unfortunately, perception is sometimes more real than reality.

Will: How's this for reality. My dad always said the company would put a family out of their camp house in the middle of the night in February if they stepped out of line. Is that true?

Clive: Is it true that striking miners would dynamite the railroads tracks? I heard tell the miners once broke into the company store and looted it. They said the only thing left in the meat department was one roll of sausage.

Will: Wonder how that roll of sausage got overlooked? I don't know if I should tell this. Well, why not? It was a long time ago.

Clive: Go ahead.

Will: When I was a boy, we didn't have much. So we only had meat a couple of times a week. Of course, you'd know that. We could afford to eat sausage for breakfast only on Sunday morning. I couldn't understand why we started having sausage every morning for a month.

Clive: I should deduct $100 from the land sale for sausage.

Will: Another thing. My brothers and me got one pair of boots a year. But one year our closet was full of new shoes and boots. My brothers and me had more than one fight over a particular pair of shoes. I think they were penny loafers.

Clive: Like I said, there's enough blame to go around.

Will: Yeah, but I'd place about 90 percent of the blame at the company's feet.

Clive: According to you, a pancake has only one side. When are we going to stop the blame game?

Will: You're pretty good at it yourself.

Clive: Your right. It's easy to fall back into old patterns. Now back to the houses.

*Will***:** So the house can't be sold out from under a man?

Clive: A man living in the house has first choice. There's about two dozen empty houses scattered throughout the camp. A man can put in a claim for one of the empties if he doesn't like his own house or if it's

34

not big enough. Will, a new day has dawned. But it'll take both sides willing to change to make it work.

Will: We'll see.

Clive: That's one thing we can all agree on.

Will: What's that?

Clive: That we'll see. (Lights fade)

Scene Five

Lights rise at suppertime in Fancy Hollow as pans of food warm on the stove. Thalia, Ollie and Hankins sit down at the kitchen table.

An unlit pipe dangles from Hankins's mouth as he reads the Bible. Thalia looks out the window pondering Jesse's comments, while Ollie slouches in his chair eying his empty dinner plate.

Although there are only three of them in the cabin, the presence of someone or something is troubling. The stove's flickering flames lend shadows to the far wall. One shadow looks roughly like a hangman's noose; the others are a hodgepodge of weird shapes. Finally, Ollie shoves back from the table and speaks.

Ollie: I thought Dad was just going to the post office. He's been gone three hours.

Hankins: The truck might've broke down. It's been acting up lately.

Ollie: One of the Johnson boys, Herbert, says he'll sell his truck. It ain't but five years old, and it's got new tires on the front.

Thalia: The last time Will and I got out of Harlan County we had one flat a going and one a coming.

Hankins: Will ain't one to give up on a tire too quick. When one of his tires gives out, he takes it personal.

Ollie: Mom, you deserve better. You need a nice car to take to town.

Hankins: This road would tear a car to pieces because of the ruts. Need something that sits up high.

Ollie: I love a Jeep and you would too Mom. Dad could give me the truck.

Hankins: You can't court a pretty girl in that thing. She'd be afraid the ugly would rub off on her.

Ollie: Granddad, I'm serious. Mom, you promised you'd talk to Dad. Don't let him sway you because he don't care about anybody but himself.

Thalia: That's enough of that talk. You don't run down your father.

Ollie: You promised.

Thalia: Ollie, go fetch some firewood. It'll be cold tonight. I'm getting where I hate to wake up to a cold house.

*Hankin*s: I hate getting up before sunlight.

Thalia: No reason for you to. You've earned a rest after working the mines.

Hankins: Oh, there ain't much I don't enjoy at my age. I just wished I could save money like Will. But I do love a good time. My other two boys, Jasper and Clete, they're like me. They can't live on a $500 a week, but they can survive on $60 a month.

Thalia: I like Jasper and Clete. They're always cutting up and laughing about something.

The door opens and Will rushes in, swaying a little before plopping in a chair at the table. He grins sheepishly and begins to tap the table hesitantly like the rhythmically- impaired often do. He hums what sounds like a fusion of *Oh, Holy Night* and *I saw Momma Kissing Santa Claus*. When Thalia looks at Will, he stops humming and scowls.

Thalia: Did you eat? I know you've had something to drink.

Will: Had a cheeseburger and a couple beers at Henrys.

Thalia: Which one is Henry's Bar? Both bars look the same to me.

Will: Henry's has the big Schlitz sign. Turner's got the Pabst Blue Ribbon Sign.

Hankins: I wouldn't drink either beer. Both taste like dishwater.

Will: I suppose you've drank dishwater, so you know what it tastes like.

Hankins: Just trying to be civil and make conversation. You should try it sometime. I think I'll go for a walk and smoke my pipe. Smoke bothers Thalia.

Will: Everything bothers Thalia, especially me.

*Thalia***:** Those mints you've been eating are no match for the bourbon you've been drinking.

Will: Dad, if you see Ollie tell him I need him.

Thalia: Ollie went to get some logs for the stove.

Will: Logs? I saw that boy standing up on that hill we cleared two years ago when we sold all the timber. He's just standing there looking lost.

Thalia: He loves to walk the hills at night. He loves this land. I bet he's walked every square inch of it more times than you can count.

Hankins: The boy's a walker. Good for a soul to walk.

37

Will: He was looking up at the sky, like he was searching for a flying saucer. Sometimes I wonder about that boy.

Hankins: Might not been him. Could've been somebody else.

Will: Dad, looks like Ollie takes after you.

Thalia: I'm glad he does.

Will: What's that suppose to mean?

Hankins: They said when Deacon Cartwright's daddy cracked up that time, he walked the mountains for days. Doak Owens said he showed up in Hazard one afternoon and couldn't remember where he'd come from. Hazard is a two-day walk even for a young man.

Will: That whole family is touched.

Hankins: I liked Old Man Cartwright, but that Hawthorne is goofy as a run-over dog. Always using big words and him not having a clue what they mean.

Will: I swear, folks can get on a man's nerves. I'm going to bed.

Will yanks the pantry door open and searches until he finds his favorite bottle of bourbon. He frowns when he sees the bottle is half-empty. He grabs a small metal box off the top shelf and tucks it under his arm, closes and locks the bedroom door.

Hankins: I guess I hit that bottle a little hard this week.

Thalia: It's not the bottle. Something else is eating at him.

Hankins: Boy always was a brooder, like a piece was missing from the puzzle. Did the best I knew how, his mother dying less than a month after he quit school and all. Raised all three of my boys the same, but they each turned out a little different. I must've done something wrong, but I swear I don't know what.

Thalia: You did the best you could. You know he's never loved me like a husband should love a wife.

Hankins: I don't know about that. For better or worse. That's what the Good Book says.

Thalia: You don't know what it says if you don't read it.

Hankins: A man would be a fool not to care for a woman like you. I love my three boys, but I always wanted a daughter. You're that daughter.

Thalia: He married me for daddy's land and we both know it. He knows it too even if he don't know it.

Hankins: You're the best thing that ever happened to him.

Thalia: I just wish for once he'd put his arm around Ollie and say he loves him. That would do the boy more good than anything.

Hankins: Something I've been meaning to tell you. I wanted to tell Ollie first, but I got to get it off my chest. I've been thinking about moving to town. I want to buy the old camp house where I raised my family.

Thalia: That's impossible. Company owns everything in Hoedown. If the Good Lord didn't own your soul, they'd own it too.

Hankins: Ain't that so.

Thalia: Do you really want to leave? Ollie and I need you because you brighten up this place.

Hankins: I talk too much. I talk too much about the past and it gets on Will's nerves.

Thalia: Young people need to learn about the past. How the hard times made the people stronger. A lot of them don't know what real hard times are.

Hankins: I love that boy. Ollie's made his share of mistakes, but he'll find his way. There's something about him that reminds me of the men who fought for the union. The harder the times, the stronger their will. The companies beat them, tried to starve them, even shot a few, but they just wouldn't give up. I guess when you got nothing to lose, it's easier to have courage.

Thalia: Are you really thinking about moving to town?

Hankins: I hope to. That Kennedy boy running for president says the coal companies should sell the houses in the mining camps. Don't know why, but I believe him. Sarah and me, paying rent all those years and nothing to show for it. I can feel Sarah looking down from above and telling me how to fix things up. We didn't have much, but Sarah was forever shuffling the furniture around trying to make things look better.

Thalia: Ollie could help you. He's good with his hands.

Hankins: Ollie's pretty handy but Will's more dangerous with a hammer than a drunkard with a loaded shotgun.

Thalia: There's nothing wrong with dreaming. When a man loses his dreams, it's like a part of him steps outside the body to taunt him.

Hankins: Yeah, kind of like a ghost.

Thalia: Like a shadow. (Lights fade)

Act Two
Scene One

Lights rise in the cabin the next morning when Will comes back from town. He opens the pantry to remove the small metal box and discovers the lid is bent and the lock damaged. He slams the pantry door so hard something falls off a shelf, and he tosses the box on the table scratching the finish. Ollie enters the front door of the cabin and hesitates when he sees Will sitting at the table.

Will: Where you been?

Ollie: On the west side of the property marking trees. Lots of popular, oak, some cedar. All good for mining timbers.

Will: Oak is stronger, poplar lighter and easier to handle. Both make good mine timbers, but I want to keep the cedars.

Ollie: Mom loves cedar. Says it keeps the moths away. I could build her a cedar chest for Christmas and do the work in the shed. She won't know a thing.

Will: Uh, about that timber-we don't want to drive too hard a bargain and back the company in a corner. Give and take is the best way to negotiate. But timbers isn't exactly what's on my mind right now.

Ollie: Dad, if the company thinks you're desperate, they'll offer almost nothing. If they can save a nickel a truckload, they'll buy elsewhere.

*Will***:** I keep getting sidetracked with timbers. This box on the table is what I want to talk about.

Ollie: What about it?

Will: The lock is broken. This is my personal papers in here. Nobody's business but mine.

Ollie: It's not Mom's business? She's worked like a dog for years helping keep this place running, but somehow it's just your business.

Will: That's not exactly what I meant. Did you break this lock or not?

Ollie: Break the lock? What are you talking about?

Will: Somebody broke the lock on this box.

Ollie: Why would somebody break the lock? What's so important about the papers in that box?

Will: Things I wasn't ready for anyone to see. Not until I explained first.

Ollie: I don't get it. Wait a minute-I do get it. It's something about the land isn't it?

Will: It's not official. I haven't made up my mind about anything.

Ollie: Lately, you've been acting sneaky, trying to keep things from us.

Will: I was waiting until the time was right.

Ollie: The right time to tell your family nothing but money means anything? That family, land, memories, nothing matters. When was the last time you visited Little Corey's grave?

Will: I'm just researching the matter. I wanted to hear an offer. It doesn't mean I have to sell. It'll just give us some idea of what the land is worth.

Ollie: You mean give you an idea what the land is worth. You've already made up your mind. I can see it in your eyes.

Will: You live in a dream world like your mother.

Ollie: You think she's silly because she dreams of being an artist. Selling paintings, having people know she's good at something besides washing your clothes and cooking the supper that you don't eat half the time because you'd rather be in a bar.

Will: Watch your mouth boy. You're speaking to your father.

Ollie: Half the land belongs to Mom. Sell your half.

Will: It don't work that way.

Ollie: What about Granddad? Where would he go?

Will: There's things we'll figure out along the way.

Ollie: You've already made up your mind to sell.

Will: I'm not saying I will and I'm not saying I won't.

Ollie: What kind of answer is that?

Will: I'm telling you for the last time, I've not decided yet. When I do, you'll be the first to know. Now, back to the broken lock. Did you do it or not?

*Ollie***:** I told you once and you didn't believe me. Why should I tell you again?

Will: Well, it had to be Thalia or Dad.

*Ollie***:** Granddad wouldn't do it. You know that.

*Will***:** Why would your mom do such a thing?

Ollie: Maybe the box fell off the shelf and broke.

Will: Don't give me that.

Ollie: Mom wouldn't lie for the world. She's always been truthful to me. Sometimes I wish she would lie.

Will: What are you getting at?

Ollie: Oh, nothing in particular.

Will: Have you given any more thought about vocational school?

Ollie: I ain't give it the first thought.

Will: What do you mean you ain't give it the first thought? You drop out of high school because they suspend you for three days. Three miserable days!

Ollie: They knew I didn't do it.

Will: You should've told the principal who broke into the office and stole those tests.

Ollie: The whole thing was a waste of time.

Will: Getting an education and making good use of your God-given talent is a waste of time? I don't understand you boy.

Ollie: You never tried to understand me. Not once have you asked me what I want.

Will: Alright, I'm asking now. What do you want?

Ollie: To sell all the timber on the west side of the property. Buy Mom a nice car and get me a tractor. I can use the tractor to keep the road up. Clear out the ditch and gravel the road. That way Mom won't be stuck here all winter. She could go to town on her own.

Will: Got it all figured out, ain't you?

Ollie: Then she wouldn't miss church so much. You both could go. We could learn to be a real family again like we use to be. We could be a farm family living off the land like it was meant it to be. Not tearing up the mountains like its being done.

Will: If the coal's in the ground, it's got to come out one way or the other.

Ollie: Yeah, but it's always the other way. The easy way. The cheap way. When the coal's all gone, the mountains all gone, what's left then?

Will: You've never been out of the hills, but you know all about the world.

Ollie: I know my world. And I know the world I want to live in.

Will: There's no use talking to you.

Ollie: Promise me you won't do anything until all four of us have their say.

Will: I can't make that promise.

Ollie: Can't or won't. If you've not made up your mind, you'll give us a chance to speak our piece.

Will: I'm the man of the family and I'll make the final decision. But you're right. We'll have a family meeting on the subject.

Ollie: You promise?

Will: You have my word on it. (Lights fade)

Scene Two

Lights rise at Gap Hollow Baptist church where the service has just concluded. A row of five chairs faces a podium (stage left).

During the sermon, the congregation enthusiastically applauded Pastor Collins, and even Deacon Cartwright bellowed "Amen" twice.

The pastor cited a parable in which Jesus said, "I was cold and you clothed me, I was sick and you cared for me, I was hungry and you fed me." The people had replied to Jesus that they had done no such thing. Jesus then responded, "When you do these things for others, you've done them for me."

During the alter call, one couple who contemplating divorce vowed to stop taking martial advice from in-laws. Another church member pledged to cancel a fishing trip to deliver a load of coal to an elderly church member. After the service, the pastor meets with Deacon Hawthorne to discuss church business.

Jesse stands before Hawthorne who sits in the middle chair facing him. Jesse is still clutching his worn leather Bible. Hawthorne's massive Bible looks as if it's never been opened. Jesse is exhausted, but Deacon Cartwright is upbeat.

Hawthorne: A great crowd for a Wednesday night prayer meeting. Keep it up and we just might get some of our flock back. Unfortunately, I heard the Jones family moved their letter to another church. Their tithes will be sorely missed.

Jesse: We've still got 124 members on the books, and we're averaging about 80 on Sunday morning.

Hawthorne: Yes, but we lose about a fourth of them on Sunday night. Wednesday is usually pitiful. Last Wednesday we only had 24.

Jesse: I counted 28.

Hawthorne: I'm the official counter. I've been doing it so long I seldom make a mistake.

Jesse: There's folks I'd love to see come back to church. But to be honest, there's some I'd like to see move out of state. Every time the Jones family got mad they threatened to quit tithing. People who give the least are the first ones to complain if a log is thrown in the stove.

Hawthorne: Nevertheless, it's the pastor's job to reach out to the wayward.

Jesse: Some folks left the area to look for work. Jake and Lucy Shelton and their four kids went to Cincinnati. I think he got a job at Ford. Jake never said a bad word about anybody. I hate to lose people like him.

Hawthorne: I heard his unemployment ran out and the Missus told him to get a job or get gone.

Jesse: You can't wait forever for the mines to call you back. My dad, bless his soul, planned to leave the mountains at least a dozen times. But when he'd get ready to go, he'd hear a rumor that the mines was starting up again. By the time it reopened, Dad was too broke down for the hard work. He didn't last six months.

Hawthorne: Sad indeed. Now back to our diminishing attendance. What about the Simpkins and the Blevins family? They've quit coming to church altogether. I don't think they're going anywhere.

Jesse: There's just one of me.

Hawthorne: If we can keep the church full, you might get that raise we promised you three years ago.

Jesse: That's not why I want the church filled. But frankly, I could use a raise.

Hawthorne: Well, Pastor, some of the deacons feel you aren't earning your salary because of the declining membership.

Jesse: I make $65 a week. Can't support a wife on that.

Hawthorne: Didn't you get quite a sum for your injury in that mining accident a few years ago?

Jesse: Between my medical bills and my lawyer's fees, I didn't get much. I should've got me a bluegrass lawyer.
Hawthorne: You're better off than most.

Jesse: That's the gospel truth.

Hawthorne: Speaking of marriage-some of the deacons expressed concern about your single status.

Jesse: I'm not getting married just to please Deacon Henshaw.

Hawthorne: How did you know? Never mind, but I've heard talk.

Jesse: I've done nothing wrong. Jesus, I haven't even put my arm around a woman in two years.

Hawthorne: Now, now. No need to talk about such.

Jesse: I just hate gossip. It puts an unhealthy spirit in the church.

Hawthorne: Nothing like that. Nothing like that at all. It's just the deacons have heard talk from some of the womenfolk. They think you've got a girlfriend somewhere. Some say you visit a lady friend in Lexington on occasion.

Jesse: Hogwash. A good friend of mine preaches in a little horse farm community near Lexington. I go there occasionally to ride horses and visit his church. I've been friends with him and his wife for nearly 15 years.

Hawthorne: I believe you, but some folks like to talk.

Jesse: I can't get married just to silence wagging tongues. I've always dreamed of marrying and raising a family, but I don't think it's in the cards for me.

Hawthorne: Well, just think about it.

Jesse: I always think about it. I pray about it. But the Lord hasn't told me to marry Deacon Henshaw's sister. Woman's got the loudest voice I've ever heard. She could win a hog-calling contest for sure.

Hawthorne: We'll both pray about it. Now there's a couple of other things on the agenda. We've got a bid for putting windows in the church. These new windows are made of aluminum and cost $15 each. That'll be $150 for the ten windows.

Jesse: Are they any good? We could caulk the wooden windows.

Hawthorne: But these come with storm windows. That will cut down the draft. Half the ladies in church say their feet stays cold from October to March.

Jesse: In that case, we better get new windows. Don't want a couple that's been married forty years splitting up over cold feet.

Hawthorne: Pastor, I enjoy humor as much as the next man, but…

Jesse: Sorry, Deacon, just trying to lighten things up. Everyone seems so serious. Doesn't anyone laugh anymore?

Hawthorne: Now, on to other business. For a year, we've discussed the need for better song books. We had to tape the spines of at least two dozen songbooks last month. Deacon Wheeler's brother-in-law is minister of music at a big church in Louisville. They've bought new song books.

Jesse: Do they want to sell the old books?

Hawthorne: Heavens no, but if we pick them up, we can have all 300 of them. They're probably in much better shape than what we have.

Jesse: I don't doubt it. But we don't want another song book controversy. The Hopkins left the church two years ago because their mother's favorite song wasn't in the last songbook.

Hawthorne: I remember that, but I can't recall the song.

Jesse: And the Slough's threatened to leave the church when Charley Perceval sang that song, "I Was a Drunkard, but the Lord Saved Me." They were offended because Mrs. Slough's brother was doing time in the Harlan jail for making moonshine.

Hawthorne: We can form a songbook committee and make sure all the songs are ok. You never know.

Jesse: You never know.

Hawthorne: Now, I've saved the most important business for last.

Jesse: Why do I have a feeling of dread?

Hawthorne: Again, let me say that sermon was wonderful. That was clever.

Jesse: Am I missing something? It wasn't a particularly good sermon.

Hawthorne: Let's just say I'm rather perceptive. I sensed there were two messages tonight. The obvious one: Like the Apostle Paul said, true religion is helping the widow, the poor and the needy.

Jesse: I hope the point was obvious. If we love Jesus, that love is reflected in the way we treat others.

Hawthorne: Ah, yes, yes. But I think we can apply the message to the controversy in the church.

Jesse: What controversy? We've always had minors problems. It's called the real world. As long as we have imperfect people, we'll have imperfect churches.

Hawthorne: Perhaps I've assumed too much.

Jesse: I'm in the dark here.

Hawthorne: You mean your message wasn't a somewhat subtle reference to the land dispute. Pastor, surely you know the church is divided about whether members should sell their land to the coal company? The company is offering decent money for land that is practically worthless for farming.

Jesse: I can't advise members one way or the other. I own eight acres that I'm not selling.

Hawthorne: Your land is on the other side of Hoedown. I doubt there would be much demand for it. But if you could encourage the five families in our church to sell, I think the company would be greatly interested in your eight acres at a fair price, if you know what I mean.

Jesse: I know exactly what you mean. How could I do such a thing? But I've thought about asking Will Poser to advise our members. He has a good head for business.

Hawthorne: Will's a little rough around the edges to suit me. But he has done well for himself. He sure doesn't throw his money away.

Jesse: We all have our flaws. Some are just easier to see than others.

Hawthorne: Pastor, I'm quite aware of your flaws. I suppose I haven't quite forgiven you for shoving me against the wall that time. Ten church members left because of you. A Preacher, a so-called man of God, attacking chairman of the deacons!

Jesse: You met me halfway, if I remember correctly.

Hawthorne: Inexcusable! I would've filed charges, but I wanted to avoid hurting the church. It's things like that that breaks a church apart. It's letting Satan in the back door. No! Inviting him in the front door!

Jesse: If I remember correctly, my predecessor once slapped you.

Hawthorne: Inexcusable!

Jesse: And that Ratliff man-can't recall his first name, the one that moved to Hazard, wasn't he chairman of the deacons at one time?

Hawthorne: Uh, why do you ask?

Jesse: Didn't he choke you during an argument about whether to have a foot washing in May or October?

Hawthorne: I'm not on trial here.

Jesse: I offered to resign but the deacons voted five to one for me to stay. Wonder who cast that negative vote?

Hawthorne: Sorry, but a secret vote must remain secret.

Jesse: I'm not proud of losing my temper. We both were at fault, but me more so, because I'm the pastor and God demand's a higher level of accountability from me. I've failed the Lord before, and I'll do it again.

Hawthorne: I was just conducting an investigation and you assumed I was accusing you.

Jesse: You told the deacons I was having an affair with a married woman.

Hawthorne: I did no such thing. I simply reported to them the talk that I'd heard. I never really believed it.

Jesse: I'll tell you one more time and you are never to speak of this again. Understood?

Hawthorne: Ah, yes.

Jesse: Mrs. Poser, uh, Thalia and I were engaged to be married. Her father didn't approve of me. I didn't want to drive a wedge between a father and his only daughter. His wife died less than a year before. I cared for Thalia very much, but I left the county for three years. When I returned for my mother's funeral, I decided to stay. I respect Thalia. I respect her family. I respect her marriage. I'm just a friend to her as a pastor. Nothing more.

Hawthorne: I believed you the first time. You simply misunderstood.

Jesse: If word had gotten back to Will or Ollie, I'm afraid you might've had to move to Tennessee.

Hawthorne: I'll never leave Harlan County.

Jesse: Hawthorne, you've resented me from the start. Why?

Hawthorne: I was willing to give you a chance. This church means a great deal to me. It's my whole life. You don't know what it's like to go home to an empty house every night. She's been gone nine years and I still hope she's there when I get back from church on Sunday night. It never ends. It never ends. It just won't stop hurting.

Jesse: I know what it's like to be alone.

Hawthorne: But you've always been alone.

Jesse: Not really.

Hawthorne: But you were never married. Myra left the day after my youngest boy, Lester, graduated from high school. The very next day she left me for a bum. A bum! He didn't even have a good muffler on the truck he drove her away in. He had nothing! Why? Why? Why?

Jesse steps toward Hawthorne and gives him a powerful hug. Completely surprised by Jesse's display of affection, Hawthorne coughs several times before regaining his composure.

Hawthorne: Uh, hum, Pastor. There is something else we need to discuss. The company has almost completed building a refuse dam at the mouth of the hollow. I'm sure you realize our little church would be in the direct path if the dam broke.

Jesse: I'm no engineer, but the dam appears to be well-built. They even put in a concrete spillway.

Hawthorne: But if it rains 40 days and nights, the church will float off like Noah's ark.

Jesse: Should we talk to the company?

Hawthorne: They'll do whatever they want. But during a deacon's meeting last month we…

Jesse: There was a deacon's meeting last month when I was out of town?

Hawthorne: Just an informal get-together.

Jesse: That violates the church's bylaws. I'm supposed to be informed of all scheduled deacon's meetings a week in advance. You know I attend as many as I can.

Hawthorne: As I say, informal, nothing more. But we discussed the possibility of selling the church property. If we get a good price, we could build in a new location: bigger church, larger membership, paved roads. Might be best for all around.

Jesse: Isn't there a two-acre tract of land across the street from your grocery store where a church burned down years ago.

Hawthorne: Why, yes.

Jesse: Doesn't one of your sons in- law own that land?

Hawthorne: Says who?

Jesse: That's what Doak Owens said.

Hawthorne: Blasted blabbermouth! Nevertheless, it would make a great location for a church. Something to think about.

Jesse: Tonight you've given me quiet a bit to think about. (Lights fade)

Scene Three

It is daylight when lights rise in the kitchen. Only Thalia and Hankins are up and moving about. Thalia sets two coffee cups on the table while Hankins tosses a log in the stove before they sit down.

Hankins: Sleep ok?

Thalia: I fell asleep soon as my head touched the pillow, but I woke every hour on the hour. I guess I'm worried about Ollie.

Hankins: You need to quit worrying so much about that boy. He's just starting to grow up. When will he be 17?

Thalia: His birthday is in August. August the 13th.

Hankins: So what's got you so worked up?

Thalia: He's changing too quickly. One day he's a sweet kid, and the next he's full of I don't know what. He can't stand to be around his father. Plus, he's got into three fights this year.

Hankins: Ollie won two of the three fights, and he never started any of them. That should count for something.

Thalia: That counts for nothing. But something else is bothering me. There's a different feel to the air. Something is creeping toward this family and I don't know what it is. I keep thinking if I can figure it out, it won't come about. Don't make much sense does it?

Hankins: You got too much on your mind. Trying to reason with my son will make you swimmy-headed. You should enjoy the morning. That first cup of coffee when everything's so peaceful with no dogs yapping. I always like to be up first. Makes me think I've got a head start on everybody else, even though I don't have much to do.

Thalia: You better enjoy the quiet while you can.

Hankins: Ollie will know it's not your idea.

Thalia: I know what Will's up to. I pried the lid off the metal box he keeps in the pantry. Will totes it around like he's carrying the secret recipe to the Colonel's fried chicken. I meant to talk to Ollie last night but I never got the chance. I have to break the news to him before somebody else does. He won't take it too well.

Hankins: Bad news is easier to take come daylight. Best not to go to bed mad though. Me and Sarah, we never went to bed mad. Ain't good for a marriage.

Thalia: I wouldn't know.

Hankins: We'd fight like Grant and Lee, but come bedtime, even if I was right, I'd say I was wrong. Wake up the next morning and eat gravy, biscuits, ham and fried apples. Sometimes, you bend so the marriage don't break.

Thalia: Why didn't you teach that to Will?

Hankins: Will's a leaky vessel. No matter how much I poured in, I wasn't sure how much leaked out. But he wasn't always like that. Will was a fun-loving, happy kid with a slew of friends. When I'd come home from the mines, they'd always be a passel of kids playing football in the front yard. Our camphouse was on a curve in the road so we had the biggest yard on our street. We never had a blade of grass in the yard even in summer, but I told Sarah it don't matter because it was the coal company's yard anyway.

Thalia: What happened to change Will?

Hankins: Uh, has Will heard any more about the company selling the camp houses?

Thalia: Will says it's a done deal. The company's got a story in tomorrow's newspaper about it.

Hankins: I've prayed the Good Lord will help me buy the old home place back. Going to put everything back like Sarah had it. You think she'll know?

Thalia: Somehow, she'll know.

Hankins: First thing, I'll hang pictures. Pictures of our wedding, first anniversary and a picture of us when I got baptized. You know, she was baptized as a young girl, but she wanted us to be dunked together.

Thalia: Pictures on the wall makes a house a home.

Hankins: You know she wouldn't marry me until I got saved. She kept after me and I just wouldn't do it. Finally, I joined a Primitive Baptist Church.

Thalia: I didn't know you were Primitive.

Hankins: My dad was too until he had a falling out with the preacher and joined an independent Baptist Church.

Thalia: What did they fall out over?

Hankins: It must've been something serious, but I never could figure it out. But that preacher kept after me until I said I'd give up fighting, drinking and cussing, but I'd be danged if I'd give up my pipe.

Thalia: I didn't know you were a heavy drinker.

Hankins: Honey, I drank enough bad liquor to crack the hull of a battleship. Anyhow, the preacher said he couldn't recall the Lord speaking against smoking a pipe, so he reckoned it was alright.

Thalia: Did you ever love anyone besides Sarah?

Hankins: Lord no. After that first date, I was caught hook, line and sinker. I remember our first date like it was last month.

Thalia: You went to the store yesterday and forgot half the things I told you to get.

Hankins: I remember how Sarah and me sat on their porch swing on that first date. It was in middle October when the leaves had peaked. The day was so pretty it made you kind of sad because you knew what was just around the corner. Anyhow, her dad, old man Rupert Wheeler, was a rascal. He made Sarah's brothers, Ogden and Hurley, set on the porch with us. Rupert said to tell him if I as much as put my arm around her. The old man was a scufller. He claimed he never started a fight in his life, but I heard he never lost one neither. I didn't care to find out.

Thalia: I never knew much about him.

Hankins: Wasn't much to know. Ogden said if I'd give him a nickel him and Hurley would go stay behind the barn. Promised not to say a word.

Thalia: Did you give him a nickel?

Hankins: All I had was a dime and he said he'd bring the change right back.

Thalia: Did you get your change?

Hankins: It's been 45 years and I ain't got that nickel yet. Ogden took my dime, run in the back door and told Rupert I was getting fresh with Sarah. The old man grabbed me by the overalls and threw me over the banister rail.

Thalia: Were you hurt?

Hankins: Just my pride. I landed in some rose bushes and was scratched something awful. Finally, Rupert calmed down and had the boys cut me lose. Those rascals cut both galleasses off my best pair of overalls.

Thalia: Those memories make life worth living.

Hankins: Funny thing though. As time eases on by, I can hardly remember the bad times. I know there was plenty, but I recall mostly the good ones. Even the bad ones seem sort of good after enough time passes.

Thalia: I'll miss this cabin, but the hardest part is leaving Little Corey's grave. According to that letter Will won't let out of his sight, the company only wants nineteen acres. That leaves some of the woods and the family cemetery.

Hankins: Well, life changes just like the seasons.

Thalia: Will and I should've had another baby. It's not right for a boy to grow up without brothers and sisters. Those two miscarriages after Coy's death scared me off. Now, It's like there's always been something left out of Ollie.

Hankins: I'll miss you and Ollie. If they ever get the road fixed you could visit me.

Thalia: Will to. Maybe things will be better back in town, but living in town will be hard for Ollie.

Hankins: Keep him out of the pool hall. He gets in a fight every time he plays a game of pool.

Thalia: I'm counting on you to talk to him about school. If he passes the GED, he can enroll in that community college in Cumberland. They say if you do good there, the university in Lexington will take you.

Hankins: Wouldn't that be something. A Poser going to college. Wonder what Sarah would think about it?

Thalia: I hear Will getting up. He's supposed to go see Clive McAlister this morning. (Lights fade)

Scene Four

Lights rise in McAlister's office where he sits at his desk shuffling papers. He stands, yawns and stretches, before going to the window and peering into the valley below. When Will arrives at company headquarters, Clive's secretary immediately escorts him into the superintendent's office. Clive turns and motions for him to sit down. Clive plops in his chair behind the desk and grabs a sheet of paper. He is smiling.

Will: The secretary told me to come on in.

Clive: Of course. Make yourself comfortable and I'll have my secretary get us coffee. Lord, my desk is a mess. I've been doing reports all morning. If it wasn't for all the paperwork, I'd have the best job in the county. The paperwork keeps me from doing real work.

Will: So what's the best part of your job?

Clive: Would you believe watching that new mining machine eat up a wall of coal and seeing it head to the conveyor belt, then to the rail cars. You should see it. It's called a continuous miner.

Will: Funny name for a mining machine.

Clive: Some fool gave it that name. But you better stop the equipment long enough to oil and grease it. If you take care of the equipment, it will take care of production. Preventative maintenance is something I've preached everywhere I've worked.

Will: That's a big change from when I worked for the company. My boss thought if you serviced the equipment, you was pampering it.

Clive: You should see this machine. Two giant cutting heads, arms that gather the coal, conveyor belt mounted on a boom. Load a coal car before you can say scat.

Will: So this is the machine that put a dozen men out of work.

Clive: It's the future. The greater production, the more company profits, the better a miner's wages and pension.

Will: So that's the way it's suppose to work.

Clive: Blasting the coal and having men loading with shovels is a thing of the past. If the industry doesn't adapt to newer and better technology, we'll lose out to oil. Mark my words, some day gas will be a dollar a gallon.

Will: Gas is 20 cents a gallon now. It'll be 100 years before it's 50 cents. I hope you don't think I'm naïve for selling my land. Nothing is going to change.

Clive: You've decided not to sell?

Will: No, I'm selling because it's a fair price for the land, not because I believe the coal industry cares about anything but profits.

Clive: So $17,000 for 19 acres is acceptable?

Will: Almost. Since you're leaving me with six useless acres, I'll need a road up the hill to the family cemetery.

Clive: You're asking a lot.

Will: My wife, son and dad are opposed to selling the land. If you put in an access road and move my cabin and barn up the hill, that might win them over. You do that and we have a bargain.

Clive: I'll have to get it approved from headquarters. But this is my proposal. We'll cut a road for you and move your cabin, but you take care of that old barn. It's not worth moving.

Will: If you give me time to move it, we've got a deal.

Clive: Not quite. I want to buy the property where that little church is located. I don't foresee any problems with the dam, but it's being built at the mouth of the hollow. Just to be on the safe side...

Will: So what's the problem?

Clive: If we had a severe flood like a decade ago, it would be risky. Better to ere on the side of safety.

Will: Their land means a lot to them. Some of these folks claim land grants almost back to the Civil War. Some will never agree to sell.

Clive: All I ask is that you try. Here's the form to sign for your check for $17,000. That's a lot of money.

Will: I feel sad all of a sudden. Wonder how money can have so much power over people? Kind of like 30 pieces of silver. Huh?

Clive: I don't get you.

Will: Never mind.

Clive: Do we need to shake on it?

Will: I gave my word and that's better than any handshake. (Lights fade)

Scene Five

It's suppertime at the cabin when the lights rise. Hankins is taking a nap in his bedroom, Will snoozes on the couch and Ollie is in the barn. Thalia has prepared a wonderful supper: fried chicken, green beans, slaw, cornbread and her specialty, deep-dish apple pie. Thalia hopes the feast might help create a calm atmosphere. She sits down only after Will and Hankins is seated. Five minutes later, Ollie lunges through the door as if someone or something is chasing him.

Ollie: Man I'm hungry. I could almost smell fried chicken in the barn.

Thalia: We'll eat after you wash those dirty hands and we say grace. Hankins, would you please say grace.

Will: The food will be cold by the time he gets through.

Hankins: Will, you could find fault with the Good Lord.

Will: Dad, it's just that you go on forever. You'll even thank the Lord for your pouch of pipe tobacco.

Hankins: We all got something to be thankful for. Were you able to wake up this morning and get out of bed?

Will: I'm here ain't I?

Hankins: Then you've got something to be thankful for. Thalia, honey, you say grace. I feel like the Lord listens more when you pray.

Thalia: Will!

Will: Sorry Dad, I'm a little frazzled. It's just when you pray it turns into a sermon. I think the Good Lord gets tired of hearing us yak.

Ollie: Good grief! I'll say grace. Why do we have to go through this every time? Why can't we just go ahead and eat?

Thalia: You're not saying grace in that tone of voice. Don't start turning into your father. One is enough.

Will: What do you mean by that?

Ollie: Will somebody please pray? I'm starving.

Thalia: I'll say grace. Heavenly father, we give thanks for all our blessings. Bless this meal and this house and all those in it. Forgive us our trespasses. Teach us to forgive one another and learn to live in peace. Amen.

Will: Live in peace?

Hankins: The Good Lord loves a simple prayer that comes from the heart. Don't need fancy words when you're talking to the Lord.

Will: Short and sweet.

Thalia: Will!

Hankins: Everybody dig in.

Ollie: Hey Dad, can I have a breast? If there's two?

Will: How many breasts do you figure a chicken has?

Hankins: I like wings and legs best. White meat is too dry.

Will: Alright Dad, we know you like the breast.

Thalia: Shut up, Will!

Ollie: Hey, what's going on? Dad, why are you being so rude? I mean more rude than you usually are.

Thalia: Everyone just eat.

Hankins: Will, can't you feel good without making everyone around you feel bad?

Will: It's not against the law for you to move out.

Ollie: How can you talk to your own dad that way? It's granddad's home just as much as it is yours.

Will: Really?

Hankins: How much did you have to drink at Henry's Bar?

Will: Apparently not enough.

Ollie: I need a drink myself.

Will: We all need a drink.

Thalia: Will, I'll crack you in the head with a skillet one of these days.

Will: I'm just kidding. Can't anybody take a joke?

Thalia: Why do you only laugh when something hurts somebody?

Will: I'll just not talk at all. How about that?

Thalia: That would be a gift from heaven.

Ollie: Granddad, I forget to tell you, you got a letter from one of your old buddies.

Hankins: Which one? Was it Ike?

Ollie: Yeah, Ike Fleenor.

Hankins: Lord, have mercy. Ike Fleenor. I ain't seen him since his kids moved him to Akron. I heard he was feeling poorly. He had more guts than any little man I know. When we was organizing our first union mine in Harlan County, he was on the other side. We laughed at him because he was the puniest company guard you ever did see. He carried a big long pistol, a shotgun and a lunch bucket big enough to feed four fat men. Ike must've had a hollow leg because he never got full.

Ollie: I've never heard you talk much about Ike.

Will: Stick around and you'll hear it a hundred times.

Thalia: Will!

Hankins ignores Will, lights his pipe and puffs several times before getting the fire stoked.

Hankins: Anyway, Ike's job was to guard the railroad tracks. That year January was mild but February was a doozy. It barely got above ten degrees the whole month. The miners' kids would grab a granny sack and sneak out at night to pick up coal that spilled off the railroad cars along the tracks. It was Ike's job to arrest them.

But Ike would go inside the guard shack and turn out the lights so he couldn't see anything. Next morning he'd tell the day boss he got so cold he shoveled the spilled coal back into the rail cars.

Ollie: Did his boss believe him?

Hankins: I guess not. They fired him eventually.

Will: Beautiful story. I'm going to cry.

Thalia: Will, I don't understand you. When your drink beer you're obnoxious. But when you drink liquor, you're cruel. Maybe it brings out the real you. Maybe it's not the liquor at all.

Ollie: Why did they fire him?

Hankins: It's a long story.

Will: Go ahead. It's still early. Tell us about how you were John L. Lewis's right-hand man. If you old-timers spilled as much blood fighting as you claim, all the mines would've been organized in three weeks, not ten years.
(John. L. Lewis was the revered labor leader that unionized the coal industry during the 30's and 40's in the Appalachian coalfields.)

Thalia: Will, exactly what heroic deed did you perform when you were a miner?

Will: Done a lot more than I got credit for.

Ollie: Granddad, finish telling about Ike.

Hankins: He caught me doing something. I ain't proud of what I done but you got to remember, we were hungry. I mean, real hungry. Somewhere along the way, hunger makes you mad. Crazy mad. I hadn't reached that point, but I was getting close. I had to do something.

Ollie: What did you do Granddad?

Will: Tell us all what you did.

Hankins glances at Will, shakes his head slowly, and then continues. He has endured Will's barbs for so long they've lost most of their sting.

Hankins: Like I said, we was facing tough times. That year nobody put out a garden for lack of seeds. The company cut off credit at the company store. But they didn't kick us out of the camphouses because they'd need us when the strike was over whether we won or not. But they knew we was close to giving up because our kids was going without.

That mine superintendent hated a union worse than the devil hates a church revival. But that rascal was born with a green thumb. He loved gardening almost as much as he loved firing a man with six hungry kids. The company police hauled cow manure to the superintendent's garden down the hill about 100 feet from his house. I swear the corn would grow at least eight feet tall and the tomatoes looked like red cantaloupes to a hungry man. I just had to get in that garden.

After Ike got moved from guarding the rails-they'd suspected him of sleeping-he was sent to guard the superintendent's house. So I waited until it stormed one night and I sneaked into the garden. I was soaked to the bone, but I loaded that sack with cucumbers, corn, cabbage, tomatoes and whatnot. I tried hard not to damage the plants but it was awful dark. When Sarah and the boys woke up the next morning, I fixed tomato gravy.

Ollie: Did you get caught?

Hankins: Here's the part that made Ike and me friends for life. I had on these funny-looking boots that made tracks in the mud like snow tires. I got them from …well, never mind. That night when I got home, those boots were soaking wet and I kicked them off in the floor right by the couch. One of the boots was lying sideways and sticking out from under the couch.

Ike and another company guard knocked on our door around noon. Ike was sharp, but that other guard had a dim bulb in the attic if you know what I mean. Can't recall his name. Ike didn't say much, but his buddy said I was the culprit and when he proved it, we'd be out on the street in a heartbeat.

When I saw that boot laying halfway in the floor for the Good Lord and all the world to see; I figured I was a goner. I started worrying where I could get a truck to haul our stuff out of the camphouse.

When that other guard-Bledsoe-that's it-Bledsoe, started questioning Sarah about my whereabouts the night before, Ike, God bless his soul, stepped toward me and kicked that boot under the couch and out of sight. For a second I thought it might've been an accident. But when he looked me in the eye, I knew he knew.

Will: Dad, your story's a little different every time.

Thalia: Will, you're scared to death to learn anything.

Hankins: That 140-pound man was about the biggest man I ever knew. When we voted the union in, the company got rid of two-thirds of their guards. They thought Ike was too puny to work the mines, but it turned out he was smart as a whip. If you showed him how to fix something once, he'd remember it for the rest of his life.

Ollie: Did you ever tell?

Hankins: Not until years later. When I was union president, because Ike had been on the company's side, some of the men wanted to blackball him from the union. I said if they did, I'd resign on the spot. They kept asking me why? I said they just had to trust me about it and they did. It was twenty years before I told it.

Ollie: Why wait 20 years?

Hankins: Oh, I don't know. Sometimes telling something makes it less. Somehow keeping it quiet makes it more right, more good, more decent. Sometimes it's better to leave a good thing unsaid.

Will: Dad, the philosopher.

Thalia: Will, have you ever had an unexpressed thought?

Hankins: Lord, I've got so many stories from the past. It's a shame that young folks don't know or even want to know them. It's a way of life that's gone forever. A part of history that won't be written again.

Will: Amen, Brother Hankins.

Thalia: Will, that's enough. If you can't hold your liquor, at least hold your tongue.

A brooding silence gradually overtakes them all. No one utters a sound for a few minutes. Finally, Ollie speaks.

Ollie: Dad, I've got most of the trees cut that you wanted to take down. I left the cedar like you said. There's about six walnut and two chestnut that I left.

Will: You've done a good job. The extra money will come in handy with all the mouths I have to feed.

Thalia: Will, if you open your trap one more time, I'll...I'll.

69

Will: You'll do nothing. I'm the man of the house. I nearly broke my back working the mines at night and farming in the daytime. Become an old man by the time I was forty just for this family.

Thalia: You were an old man long before 40.

Will: What do you mean by that remark?

Thalia: Take a month and think on it.

Hankins: Now there's no need for anybody to get riled. Besides, I got some good news.

Ollie: Are you going to take that fishing trip to Florida?

Hankins: Better than that. I want to buy my old home place back.

Ollie: This is you home Granddad. Why do you want to leave? Dad, it's all your fault!

Thalia: Hankins, we love you and want you to stay.

Hankins: Everybody calm down and listen to me. Listen real good. I've been laying awake at night thinking about the old house. I know it's not much, but if the company will sell it to me, I'll buy it.

Ollie: Granddad, how could you leave this place? We've got the prettiest land around. I'd die before I'd leave it. But we'd never sell it would we Dad?

Hankins: Ollie, you could come visit me and spend the night if you was tipsy...

Thalia: What do you mean tipsy?

Hankins: I mean, if he was tired. Look, I know I'm welcome here, but I've got to get back in that house. Reckon, I don't fully understand it myself. But something is calling me back there.

Will: A miner named Tackett rented the house but he was laid off. It's been empty for a month. He must've been in a hurry because Doak Owens said he left half his stuff. Must've had the police or a bill collector chasing him.

Hankins: I'll go to the mine office tomorrow and see if they can tell me something. Tackett will likely come back with a pickup truck to get the rest of his stuff.

Will: No need for that. When I see Clive this week, I'll ask him about it.

Ollie: Clive McAlister? Why would you go see him? What business you got with the superintendent?

Will: Just personal business.

Ollie: What kind of personal business?

Will: Do I have to answer to you? Who's the head of this house anyway?

Ollie: Is it about the trees? I told you we could hold out for a better price.

Will: Huh? Trees? Oh yeah, the trees.

Ollie: I'm going to get a book on forestry and study up.

Will: Something to think about.

Ollie: This land is good for farming and for growing trees. Corn is hard for the soil, but we can rotate the crops.

Hankins: My old man wore out our land by not rotating the crops. Land too high up in the hills and didn't get enough sun. Soil up there too rocky. Still, my dad loved the land. Never did get over losing it.

Ollie: Company stole it? You're dad should've got a good lawyer. An honest lawyer.

Hankins: Ha. You'd find a gold brick at the bottom of the outhouse quicker than you'd find an honest lawyer around here. You just hope your crooked lawyer outhustles their crooked lawyer. Bless the old man's soul. He believed if a man shook his hand and gave his word that was all you needed.

Will: He was a fool.

Hankins: He was trusting. He was naïve, but he wasn't no fool.

Will: He went into business with a lawyer and a man who owned a sawmill. Five years later, the mine closes and files bankruptcy and you're daddy, my grandpa, ends up broke. His former business partners bought small farms down in the bluegrass. But your dad, my grandpa, died with nothing.

Hankins: True. Dad lost it all. But the Good Book says you come into this world with nothing and you leave with nothing.

Will: The meek shall inherit the earth-but not its mineral rights. Ha. He was a dang fool.

Hankins: Well, the Good Book says something else too.

Thalia: Haven't you heard? Will's an expert on the Bible, even though he's never read it.

Will: Know more than I let on.

Thalia: Or let on more than you know.

Ollie: What's the Bible say?

Hankins: Jeremiah 17:11, my favorite verse.

*Will***:** Go ahead and tell us Dad. You're dying to.

Hankins: Like a partridge that sittith on her eggs and
hatcheth not,
So is a man that getteth riches
and not by right,
Shall lose them in the midst of his days,
And at the end shall be a fool."

Thalia: That's beautiful.

*Ollie***:** Didn't know that was in the Bible.

Will: You're all dreamers. I'm going to bed. Where's my bottle? Dad, you ain't drank it all have you?

Hankins: It's not because I didn't give a good try.

Ollie: Don't forget Dad. Act like you've got another buyer for the timber and they'll up the ante.

Will: Dreamers. Everyone of you. Nothing but dreamers. (Lights fade)

Act Three
Scene One

A week later, lights rise in the cabin in the afternoon as Hankins and Thalia finish boxing up his belongings. Hankins bed frame and a dozen cardboard boxes are stacked against the right wall. Hankins is cheerful but Thalia is subdued. Someone knocks at the door and both yell, "Come in Pastor," in perfect timing as if they had rehearsed the greeting.

Hankins: Jesse, I'm glad you could make it. After I get my house lined out, I'll have you over for supper.

Jesse: Brother Hankins, your cooking is a half-step ahead of mine, but that ain't saying much.

Thalia: Sit down Jesse. You're making me nervous like you're about to preach. Hankins, I'll get us some coffee and apple pie.

Jesse: Don't go to no trouble.

Thalia: If it was any trouble I wouldn't do it.

.
Hankins: Thalia's just teasing. If she don't like you, you'll know it.

73

Jesse: Thalia must've missed my sermon about a woman being submissive.

Thalia: I missed that sermon about Proverbs too.

Jesse: Which sermon was that?

Thalia: The one that says even a fool is thought wise when he remains silent.

Jesse: Hankins, what are we going to do with Thalia? She needs to go down to the altar.

After Jesse's truck is loaded, Hankins takes the keys, shakes hands and promises to return the vehicle with a full tank of gas. After Hankins leaves, an awkward silence engulfs the room. When Thalia and Jesse hear the truck start, they sit down at the table.

Jesse: Thalia, I shouldn't be here. The plan was for me to drive Hankins to town.

Thalia: He agreed I should talk to you about Ollie.

Jesse: I'm uncomfortable with just the two of us here.

Thalia: We can let the mule in the kitchen if it'd make you feel better.

Jesse: Thalia, you're something else.

Thalia: Jesse, this is not about you or me. This is about Ollie and I need help.

Jesse: What can I do?

Thalia: Maybe Ollie will listen to you. I'm worried about him and this obsession with the land. He loves it too much. It's too much a part of him.

Jesse: So Will's gone and done it and not told Ollie. Has the contract been signed yet?

Thalia: It's now officially their land. Maybe its always been their land but we didn't know it. Years ago, when we built this home place, it didn't feel like it was ours for an eternity. It seemed like we were still renting a camphouse in Hoedown. Maybe you never really own anything in this world. Wonder if the coal companies feel the same way?

Jesse: What do you mean?

Thalia: They've taken a million tons of coal out of the ground, but do they feel like the land still belongs to the Indians?

Jesse: I doubt it. Some companies have their own version of the golden rule. Since they've got the gold, they make the rule.

Thalia: Jesse, I'll be honest with you. I've never been afraid of much, but right now I'm scared to death. Something is coming to our door and I'm afraid to open it. I've never felt like this before.

Jesse: Sometimes, I feel that way late at night. It's scary but alluring at the same time. Remember that time we took a canoe trip down the Big Sandy River?

Thalia: I'll never forget that day. The sky was so pretty I thought that heaven had to be the same shade of blue.

Jesse: It rained three straight days before the trip. When we started downriver, the water was so swift the trees seem to fly by. We went around in circles and the harder we paddled the farther we got from shore. Funny thing though. A part of me wanted to rush ahead and embrace the unknown. Its like the river's will was stronger than mine. Now, I feel that same way again. I want to embrace what's coming, but at the same time run away fast as I can.

Thalia: Has Deacon Cartwright finally run you crazy?

Jesse: I use to have all the answers, but now I'm not even sure what the questions are. Lord, Thalia, what's going on?

Thalia: Jesse, whether you want to or not, we're going to have a heart to heart talk for the first time in over 20 years. You said you left because the five acres was lost, but there's another reason. There's something that else you're not telling me.

Jesse: I don't know what you talking about.

Thalia: I've always heard a rumor.

Jesse: Don't believe everything Doak Owens says.

Thalia: Well, I'll tell you so you won't have to lie.

Jesse: I've got my faults, but I don't lie.

Thalia: Except to yourself.

Jesse: All right, Thalia, you tell me what happened.

Thalia: You caught one of the Johnson boys, Harley, I think, and threatened him. He told you my daddy loaned him and his brothers the money to buy that land. You went looking for Daddy and found him sitting in church. Daddy saw you standing in the rain peering through the window but you ran away. They found your rifle outside leaning against the church wall. You just up and ran away.

Caught off guard, Jesse stares at the grounds in his empty coffee cup. When silence becomes a burden, he speaks, hoping to take the conversation in a different direction.

Jesse: Uh, uh, Thalia, how soon do you have to be out?

Thalia: Six weeks and I need to tell Ollie before he finds out elsewhere. I'm afraid he'll do something crazy. I want him to get away from here, even though it will break my heart. Families are meant to stay together, but we never got it right from the start

Look at our neighbors, the Callahan's. They sold their land and now the youngest boy is in the army, the girl is married and living in California, and the oldest boy is working in Detroit. The whole family hasn't been together in years.

Jesse: Where would Ollie go? I can't imagine him not living in Fancy Hollow. I hate to see folks sell their land because it's never the same afterwards.

Thalia: When I was a little girl, some families owned as much as 40, 50, even 60 acres. It's all gone now. But things have to change. Will is always saying we mountain people are our own worst enemies because we fight change so hard. Ollie has to change too. I want him to go to that community college they opened in Cumberland last fall. It's the best thing to happen to Harlan County.

Jesse: Second best thing.

Thalia: What do you mean?

Jesse: You're the best thing that ever happened to Harlan County.

Thalia: Promise me you'll talk to him.

Jesse: You've got my word on it. Now I want to talk to you about something. I want you to come back to church.

*Thalia***:** Why should I? I can read my Bible at home. On Sunday, I sing until it drives Will half-crazy. Part of the reason I do it.

Jesse: I want you to hear me preach one last time.

Thalia: One last time! Are you leaving? Where would you go?

Jesse: Maybe nowhere but I'm not sure. But there's one thing I'm sure of.

Thalia: Uh, what might that be?

Jesse: I've decided to give my house and land away.

Thalia: Are you crazy?

Jesse: There's a good chance of that. But I want you and Ollie to have my house and land. The house isn't enough to get stuck up about, but it's eight of the prettiest acres you'll see in Harlan County.

Thalia: Why would you do such a foolish thing?

Jesse: Ollie having his own land might help him adjust. He can't live with people so close he can reach out his window and shake hands with his neighbor who's sitting on the couch.

Thalia: Will would be livid. For all his faults, and God knows there's a few, he's proud of being a breadwinner.

Jesse: It has to remain a secret between you two. I don't want Will thinking I'm undermining his marriage.

Thalia: He's done that all by himself. But I'll do it if you'll do something for me.

Jesse: Well, I guess, ok.

Thalia: Tell me how you feel about me.

Jesse: I, uh, don't know what you mean?

Thalia: Jesse, don't be coy with me. I can see right through you.

Jesse: What good would it do?

Thalia: Just be honest and tell me how you feel.

Jesse: You're a married woman. We shouldn't talk like this.

Thalia: You speak such beautiful words about honesty, character and living with a purpose. You phony.

Jesse: You're taking my words out of context.

Thalia: Are you afraid?

Jesse: I don't have the right to tell you how I feel. I gave it up long ago.

Thalia: Tell me!

Jesse: How would it do any good? Things will still be the same.

Thalia: What you don't know about women, I could write a book.

Jesse: You belong to someone else.

Thalia: Jesse Collins, if I had my gun right now, I'd shoot you in the rear end!

Jesse: You don't know what you're asking.

Thalia: Believe me I know. Look me in the eyes and tell me I never meant anything to you.

Jesse: Thalia, please.

*Thalia***:** What's that you say almost every sermon? The truth shall set you free.

Jesse: Please don't.

Thalia: Tell me you hate me or that you don't care one way or the other. It would be easier than not knowing. That's all I ask. Nothing more.

Jesse: Thalia, I can't, I shouldn't say…

Thalia: Tell me!

Jesse: Thalia, please!

Thalia: You talk about love like you've got a glass wall surrounding you.

Jesse: Thalia, you don't know...

Thalia: Are you incapable of love. Maybe you're like someone who talks about the joy of singing when they've never sang in their life.

Jesse: Thalia.

*Thalia***:** Tell me, you coward!

Jesse: You know how I feel.

*Thalia***:** That's not good enough. I can't live not knowing. Jesse, don't you need to know if you're loved just for who you are? Not for how much you know or how much you own. Don't you need that Jesse? Oh,

Jesse, please tell me.

Jesse: You're right about truth setting you free. But truth is a sharp knife that cuts deep. Every feeling doesn't need to be spoken to be true.

Thalia: Do you want me to tell how I feel about you?
Jesse: Good Lord, no.

*Thalia***:** Then buster, you better open your heart now and speak the truth. If not, I might show up for Sunday morning service and sit in the front row. I'll wear my prettiest dress and hat, and stand up and testify how I feel about the pastor.

Jesse: Is that a threat?

Thalia: You better believe it's a threat. It's a threat, a promise, a, uh...

Jesse: You're serious aren't you? You mean every word you're saying.

Thalia: Big boy, you've got a decision to make. This is your last chance to speak truthfully to me. Otherwise, we'll never speak again, not even to say hello.

Jesse: Thalia, I can't lose your friendship.

Thalia: Then speak your peace now or you won't be welcome here again.

Once again, the sun fights through the mist and the light is dazzling. Minute dust particles dance and prance along the sunbeams. For several minutes neither speak. It's like the brief interlude of quiet, almost heavenly silence, before a dynamite blast rips tons of coal loose from the earth's grasp.

Jesse clasps Thalia's hand and is surprised by her strength. Suddenly, he emits a gut-retching squall that flows only from a tortured soul. He jerks his hand away and pounds the table with both fists before shaking them at heaven. He then looks into Thalia's unblinking, direct gaze. Tears streak his face. Jesse starts speaking softly and then his voice grows stronger.

Jesse: Thalia, I've never loved anyone like I love you. Love for church, family and friends is like hate compared to the way I feel about you. Sometimes, I go walking in the middle of the night, fall on my knees, look up at the sky and swear I'd spend eternity in hell if I could do things over again. I'd cut off my right arm if I could make you mine. Before God, I'd strangle Will with my bare hands if you could be mine again!

Thalia: Oh, Jesse.

Jesse: You wanted me to speak, now listen. I told you before, I thought I could see my shadow move, like it's got a will of its own. I believe that's a part of me, outside my body searching, trying to grab hold of the one true thing in my life-that is my love for you.

Do you remember the revival last year? The church was full for three straight nights. The last night of the revival, I couldn't sleep so I got up at two o'clock and walked all night. It started pouring rain, but I just kept walking. I said you're name over and over again. Come daylight, I was standing at my front door.

Don't know how I got there. Got sick and stayed in bed three days. Now here's the strange part. You came to take care of me. But it couldn't have been you. How could you know I was sick? God must have sent an angel disguised as you. Even if you were a thousand miles away, you were still there. Your soul and spirit were there. God used you to save my life.

Thalia: Oh, Lord, Jesse.

Jesse: Say I'm crazy but you nursed me back to health. I had a fever and you kept putting a cold cloth on my brow and fed me chicken soup that you made. When my fever broke, I could see clearly for the first time in my life. God showed me how it would've been so right.

Like if it was snowing, I'd rise early in the morning and get a blazing fire going so when you got up you wouldn't be cold. I know winter weather makes your knee hurt bad. That ornery horse threw you when you were what 15, 16? I'd let you stay in bed and I'd plump up your pillow and get your coffee. I know you like your coffee as soon as your foot hits the floor.

Thalia: You know me better than I know myself.

Jesse: And we'd talk about what was in our hearts, almost knowing what each other is thinking. And no one could break us apart. Somebody's always trying to bust up people who are meant to be together. But Hell can't stand against a man and woman who are best friends. I know what I've said don't make sense. But if God were to strike me dead this minute, I wouldn't take back one word. So Thalia, now you know how I feel about you.

Thalia: Jesse, please don't say another word.

Jesse: Lord, I feel like the world's been lifted off my shoulders. It's kind of funny though. The fear and worry is gone. Now I'm at peace. I feel completely free for the first time in my life.

Thalia: Oh, Jesse. (Lights fade)

Scene Two

One week later the lights rise at company headquarters in Hoedown. In attendance are Clive McAlister, Will Poser, Thurman Moberly, chief detective, and Burke Whitaker, his assistant. They are discussing acts of vandalism committed against the company the past week.

Clive: Will, it doesn't look good for your son. If Ollie is innocent, he needs to turn himself in. If he'll do that, you have my word it'll go easier for him. We'll take into account that he's a teenager.

Will: You ever heard of innocent until proven guilty? Nobody has seen Ollie do one darn thing.

Clive: He's been gone a week. Nobody knows where he is. Clemon Grover was hunting the other day and saw Ollie cutting toward a ridge back to town.

Will: Clemons's glasses are thicker than an airplane's windshield. Eyes so bad he almost shot his brother when they were deer hunting last year. That's not much of a witness.

Clive: Clemon had a pair of binoculars with him.

Will: Because someone saw Ollie doesn't mean he's done anything wrong.

Clive: Look Will, I can't blame you for taking up for your kid. Lord knows I'd do the same thing for my own. But you have to admit it looks suspicious Ollie coming home, grabbing a rifle and storming out of the house. It's not hard to figure he's up to something.

Will: I never said the boy wasn't strange. Well, that's not the word I'm looking for. He's just different. Gets that from his mother's side of the family. You know how artistic people are. They live in a dream world-a different world than we do. Ollie thinks he's another Daniel Boone. He could stay in the mountains and live off the land. He's a throwback to another generation. In a way, I admire him for it.

Clive: You admitted he was furious when he heard about the land sale. The day Ollie took off, my boy Sherman asked him if he was moving to town since you sold the land. Sherman said Ollie flew into a rage and threw a cue ball through the pool room window.

Will: Is that the way it happened? Ollie and Sherman got into a scuffle a couple of weeks ago. Ollie got the best of him. Maybe Sherman figured it was payback time.

Clive: The boys did fight, but they made peace and were playing a game of pool that afternoon. Don't make more of it than there is.

Will: You're the one making a mountain out of a mole hill.

Clive: I can sympathize with what Ollie's going through. But he has to be stopped. I'm sorry but it'll be one way or the other.

Will: I don't appreciate you threatening my son.

Clive: Now who's living in a dream world? I'm not saying Ollie is a bad kid. Good kids can do bad things. I know your boy is a hard-working, polite, respectful kid. Other than fistfights and occasional drinking, he's never given the police a problem. If he's innocent, help me to help him.

Will: I knew Ollie was upset about me selling the land. I should've told him before he found out. I figured he went camping to blow off steam. He's done that before. He'll go in the mountains by himself and come back with herbs and plants to sell. I couldn't add up the money he's made over the years selling ginseng.

Clive: Ollie's been gone a week. There's been vandalism for a week. Quite a coincidence isn't it.

Will: Have you thought about that preacher, Jesse Collins, that took off. He's been gone a week too.

Clive: He's the preacher at that little Baptist church down the hollow from where you live?

Will: Yeah and if you ask me, he's more a suspect than my boy. Nobody has seen him for a week.

Clive: I don't know much about him, so I'll let Thurman Moberly and his assistant, Burke Whitaker take it from here.

Moberly opens his folder, clears his throat, and awaits a signal from the superintendent to indicate he is through speaking. However, Whitaker squirms in his seat, chomping at the bit. The superintendent nods for Moberly to begin.

Moberly: Mr. McAlister, we've accumulated a thorough file on Ollie Poser. He's almost 17 years old and a high school dropout. He left school after the principal threatened to suspend him unless he told who stole test finals in history, biology and physics. The principal believes Ollie saw the culprits but wouldn't tell on them.

Ollie has no arrests even though he had been picked up for drinking in public. He wasn't intoxicated so the police let him go. He's been in three fistfights this past year. However, witnesses said he wasn't the instigator in any of the fights.

Will: I taught him not to start a fight, but never to back down.

Clive: Will, please. Mr. Moberly this is interesting, but cut to the chase.

Moberly: Yes Sir. The profile is of a loner, a bit high strung and someone who, when provoked, might commit such acts of violence. Also, he has an attachment to his land that's almost fanatical.

Clive: A tree hugger, huh?

Moberly: Not exactly, Sir.

Clive: Mr. Whitaker, tell us about Jesse Collins and please keep it brief. I have a meeting in an hour.

Whitaker: Yes Sir. Jesse Collins is pastor at Gap Hollow Baptist Church. He spent four years in the army where he became proficient at boxing. We've interviewed a lot of church members and only one person said he believes Collins is capable of violence.

Clive: He's been gone a week?

Whitaker: Correct. His truck is missing. It's a four-wheel vehicle with off road tires, so he can travel throughout the hills. Collins told church members he needed some time off and left the day after Ollie went missing.

Clive: Sum it up quickly, Mr. Whitaker.

Whitaker: Yes Sir. He's a loner, never been married, was engaged, but broke it off at the last minute. Collins left Harlan County for three years. When he came home, he worked the mines for eight years before suffering a neck injury from a roof fall. He received a workmen's compensation settlement and never worked the mines again.

Clive: What are his politics?

Whitaker: Collins has remained neutral about people selling their land. He hasn't expressed support or opposition to coal mining in general. Collins doesn't discuss politics from the pulpit. He's a walking contradiction.

Clive: What do you mean?

Whitaker: He's a skilled boxer, but never fights. He likes people, but seldom has a girlfriend or close friends. People like him but can't get a handle on him.

Clive: Could he do something like this?

Whitaker: Sorry Sir, but we just don't know.

Clive: This time could've been better spent. Go find Poser and Collins. And please use restraint.

Moberly: Will that be all, Sir?

Clive: One more thing. Do you have a composite list of acts of vandalism committed against our company?

Moberly: Yes Sir. They start out minor and grow progressively worse. Not a good sign. First, a chain link fence was cut in a several places. Then a company truck was hot-wired and pushed over a hill. About 16 windows were broken at the mine warehouse, 11 tires were slashed on company vehicles, a bulldozer driven into a pond. Extensive damage there. And the last act which got us worked up: dynamite, blasting caps, fuses and powder missing from a concrete bunker.

Clive: Gentlemen, this meeting is over. Find Collins and Poser. Will, I'm sorry, but if you know anything, now's the time to speak. **(Lights fade)**

Scene Three

Lights rise two hours past dawn in Hankins's camphouse. All the furniture is in place, and by the front door, (stage right) empty cardboard boxes eagerly await disposal.

Hankins, alone in his house, sleeps in a rocking chair he recently purchased. His Bible is in his lap and his unlit pipe rests in his hand. He awakens when someone walks upon the front porch. A few seconds later, a boisterous fist bangs the door. Hankins considers fetching his pistol but decides against caution. He can't imagine anyone wanting to hurt him, but still he opens the door slowly. He hopes it's Ollie but his close friend, Chester Wiggins is standing there.

Hankins: Chester, what in the world are you doing up before ten o'clock ? Did the slats fall out of the bed?

Chester: I'd feel better if they did. My back is giving me fits since the weather turned cold.

Hankins: I was hoping you were Ollie. I'm worried sick about that boy.

Chester: Well, as you can see, I ain't Ollie. But I heard he was in a heap of trouble.

Hankins: Have they found him?

Chester: No, but I ran into Will yesterday. Thalia has just about run herself crazy looking for that boy. I reckon she's out looking for him right now.

Hankins: Lord, have mercy. That's a strong-willed woman.

Chester: Tell me about it. Will said she caught him gone, packed her saddlebags, grabbed a rifle and took off on her horse. Will's so mad he can't see straight.

Hankins: He'd had to hogtie Thalia to keep her from looking for Ollie.

Chester: Ollie's a fine boy. He's just mixed up.

Hankins: What about Jesse?

Chester: He's still missing too.

Hankins: Ollie needs to give himself up. I wish he'd show up at the door right now.

Chester: That's why I'm here. To tell you what I heard at the barbershop yesterday while I was waiting to get a haircut. I heard tell Doak Owens told the barber the company was offering a reward for information about Ollie's whereabouts.

Hankins: Folks always needing money. Somebody will turn him in sooner or later.

Chester: Here's something else. They say the police has been watching your house since you moved in. They figured Ollie would finally show up.

Hankins: Have a seat while I fix some coffee.

Chester: Might as well.

Hankins: By the way, how's your brother doing? Last time I talked to him, he barely knew me.

Chester: He's getting worse. It's been three years since Bessie passed away, but Roy's still mourning. And he can't hardly catch his breath. All that coal dust he breathed over the years is finally catching up to him. It's a wonder any of us can breathe.

Hankins: It takes a while to bounce back after you lose your wife. I still think about Sarah all the time.

Chester: I don't understand it. Half the time Roy and Bessie acted like they hated each other. But me and my old woman hardly ever fussed, but we couldn't stand to be around one another.

Hankins: Folks that fuss all the time usually stay together.

Chester: They fought about every day that first year they were married. The lived above a bar in Cincinnati and made such a racket the bartender would stand on a chair and poke the ceiling with a broom handle to hush them up.

Hankins: Lived in Norwood didn't they?

Chester: Yeah, but half the people in Norwood were from Harlan, Hazard or Cumberland. I should've stayed with Ford myself, but you know how it is. Every time the mine closed, I'd go back to Cincinnati and swear I was never leaving. But I always did.

Hankins: I did the same thing. I quit Ford twice but they hired me back. They put all us mountain boys in the foundry. Figured if we'd work underground, we wouldn't complain about a foundry.

Chester: Ever wonder how life might've been different if you'd stayed in Cincinnati?

Hankins: I've thought about it some. But I figured I'd make the same mistakes again. Funny but a man can be gone from the mountains 40 years and still call it home.

Chester: I've seen folks move away when they were young. But when they died, their kids would bring them back to bury in the family cemetery.

Hankins: Something about the mountains keeps pulling us back.

Chester: I just couldn't stay gone. But you know, coal mining is a strange business. You start out hating it but it grows on you. Lord, I hated midnight shift. Every

Sunday night my wife would pack my lunch bucket and suitcase, sit both by the door, and tell me to take my pick. If I knew then what I know now, I'd picked the suitcase.

Hankins: I hated second shift. Left for work before the kids got home from school. They'd be in bed before I got home at midnight. Seemed like they grew up without me knowing it. I shouldn't worked all that overtime.

Chester: When you got hungry mouths to feed what can you do?

Hankins: It got a little easier after we voted the union in. I remember like it was yesterday. I got 40 cents an hour raise.

Chester: I got a quarter-or was it 30 cents? Why was your raise bigger?

Hankins: I was a roofbolter and you were a shuttlecar operator.

Chester: Company started everybody at roofbolting, using that drill we called a widowmaker. Used a 35 lb. torque wrench to tighten roofbolts. I still have nightmares about roofbolting.

Hankins: Roofbolting makes you strong as an ox. You could always tell a roofbolter because he'd have forearms like Popeye.

Chester: You remember that time we got letters from John L. Lewis. I thought I was the only one. Showed my letter to everybody, bragging I was his right-hand man and was getting a job at union headquarters.

Hankins: There was about 200 of those letters floating around. I kept mine for years, but misplaced it when I moved in with my son and his family.

Chester: I never did make it to Washington, D.C.

Hankins: Neither did I. We never made it to Florida to go deep-sea fishing, or to the Kentucky Derby. I always wanted to see Mammoth Cave too.

Chester: Why didn't we do the things we always planned to do?

Hankins: I guess when we finally got the money and the time, we couldn't remember why we wanted to do them in the first place.

Chester: Did you ever meet John L. Lewis?

Hankins: Never did. He was supposed to come to Harlan after we won the strike and something came up at the last minute. But I got an autographed picture of him. Ain't had time to put it on the wall yet.

Chester: I met John L. Lewis in person. I was in the hospital that first time I hurt my back. He come to Harlan to dedicate the Miners' Memorial Hospital. I'll never forget it as long as I live. He walked right into my room and shook my hand. He said what we accomplished would benefit generations to come. It brought tears to my eyes. And you know I don't ever cry. I hardly cried when Chester Junior was killed in that roof fall. Doctor said I was in shock.

Hankins: How long has it been?

Chester: Eighteen years this September. But it was different this year.

Hankins: How so?

Chester: I'm ashamed to say but I plumb forgot the day. Had a doctor's appointment and had to get my truck fixed. The carburetor was messed up. Was it wrong for me to forget?

Hankins: Lord, Chester, 18 years is a long time.

Chester: Sometimes it seems like two or three years. You know I dreamed about Junior last week.

Hankins: About him getting covered up in the roof fall?

Chester: No, I dreamed he was sitting at the foot of my bed talking to me. When he was a teenager, if he got in trouble he'd always come and tell me. He knew if I found out from somebody else first, I'd blister his britches. But in the dream I asked him why he went away and he just disappeared. Kind of strange. He was just 19 and had a lot of growing up to do. But I believe he would have made a good man. Shy around the girls though. Not like his old man.

Hankins: If you'd been a little more shy around women, you might still be married.

Chester: You know my wife never did have anything good to say about me. If I worked Saturday, she'd say I was a poor manager with my money. If I didn't work Saturday, she'd say I was too lazy to work. Anyhow, the Good Lord knew what he was doing when he made women. Women, baseball, poker, horseshoes. Overall, it's been a darn good life.

Hankins: I ain't complaining. I just wish I'd spent more time with my family, especially at church. Say, I'm getting hungry. You want some breakfast?

Chester: I better get going and check on my brother.

Hankins: Lord, have mercy. It's always something.

Chester: Ain't it though. (Lights fade)

Scene Four

Lights rise at the dam site. The stage consists of a cardboard drawing of a dam and several large boulders. It is the third week of November and the dam's construction is complete. Harley Simpkins, chief engineer, Moberly and Whitaker watch the dam slowly fill with water. The chilly weather has warmed and a light, steady rain has fallen for five consecutive days causing the swollen mountain streams to fuse into a powerful flow.

The dam is only half-full of water, but Simpkins is ecstatic about the accomplishment. However, Moberly and Whitaker, who are familiar with the ravages of poorly-constructed dams in the Appalachian coalfields, express mocking concern.

Moberly: Sure hope the dam holds with all the water pouring in.

Simpkins: You don't know much about dams. It could rain for a month and not hurt a thing. We built this one right. Clay to prevent seepage, a concrete spillway to divert an overflow.

Whitaker: I wouldn't want to be sitting in that little church down there if this thing did give away.

Simpkins: About as much chance of that happening as you sitting in that little church house.

Moberly: Burke went to church when he was young.

Whitaker: Yeah, but I quit going when I got to eighth grade. Figured I knew more than the preacher and had better things to do.

Moberly: Yeah, like drinking, fighting and stealing. Did I leave anything out?

Whitaker: Just the cussing.

Simpkins: Listen to me. See those overflow pipes about two feet from the top of the dam. That allows excess water to bleed off too. Even if the water ran over the top, the dam would still hold. This company is no small-time outfit. When we do something, we do it right. I got the most skilled engineers of any coal company around.

Moberly: The company pays them good that's for sure. Pays everybody good.

Simpkins: If things work out, this company will be here at least 40 years. This company is making a long-term commitment, not like these jack-legged operators that are here today and gone tomorrow. So it's absolutely vital that this dam is kept secure. Understand?

Moberly: A dozen company guards are combing these hills right now. We'll get Poser and Collins before long.

Simpkins: I'm going to town to meet with Mr. McAlister. The minute you catch them, call the dispatcher on your two-way radio. Good luck boys and please be careful. Mr. McAlister prefers they be brought in peacefully. We don't need any bad publicity, especially when things are going so well.

When Simpkins leaves, Moberly and Whitaker use their field glasses to canvass the area. After about 15 minutes, Whitaker points excitedly toward the west.

Whitaker: Boss I see something. It's, it's, I'm not sure. Over there by that clump of trees! Do you see anything?

Moberly: Nothing. I don't see anything.

Whitaker: Keep your eyes on that bunch of trees. I see some movement there. I know I saw something.

Moberly: Yeah, now I see it. It could ba a deer or another animal. But something is moving. Look! Look!

Whitaker: Yeah! I see! I see! It's a hunter, a man in camouflage. I bet it's Poser or Collins.

Moberly: You drive and I'll ride shotgun. I hope we can bring them in without a fight. Whoever it is.

Whitaker: Say boss, are you getting too old for this rough stuff? You may want to think about retirement.

Moberly: I've been thinking about retirement for the past ten years. But the closer I get, the farther away it seems.

Whitaker: I wouldn't mind roughing them up before we take them in. Teach them a lesson.

Moberly: You don't know much about mountain people, do you?

Whitaker: I know enough not to spend the rest of my life living here and doing this job.

Moberly: There's something else you need to know.

Whitaker: Like what?

Moberly: Treat these people with respect and it'll go a long way. Trying to bully them is the worst thing you can do. Sometimes people need to spill their guts to somebody. If they can do that, they won't be so easy to rile. And learn to be a listener. It's an undervalued asset.

Whitaker: What if they're still riled up?

Moberly: Then do what you have to do. Now remember, give them a chance to surrender. Mr. McAlister made that clear. Do you understand?

Whitaker: I understand this is going to look good on my record. We both might get a promotion or a bonus out of this. Then maybe I can get the heck out of here and back to where I belong.

Moberly: And where's that?

Whitaker: Anywhere but here. (Lights fade)

Lights rise at the dam site, where Ollie is stringing a fuse to ignite dynamite. He hesitates when he hears a branch snap, wheels toward the noise and draws his pistol.

Ollie: Preacher, I almost shot you just now! I've seen you in the woods a couple of times when you were looking for me. I could've shot you any time I wanted.

Jesse: Why didn't you shoot me?

Ollie: I've got my reasons. I like you even if you are a preacher. But that's not why I didn't shoot you.

Jesse: Ollie, if you blow the dam, they'll hunt you down and you'll likely lose your life. Your mother would never get over it.

Ollie: It's got to be done. These coal companies destroy everything. They always have and they always will.

Jesse: This isn't the right way and you know it. If you commit violence, you become what you're fighting against.

Ollie: How can you defend coal companies? They stole great granddad's land. They stole our land.

Jesse: Your dad made the decision to sell. It was a legally negotiated contract between Clive McAlister and you dad. It's over.

Ollie: It'll never be over.

Jesse: The company plans to hire 500 men right away. They'll have at least 1,000 men working when all the mines open.

Ollie: God, you're naive. They'll start out mining underground, but give them a few years and it'll be all strip-mining. Mark my words, there won't be a tree left in Harlan County if somebody don't stop them. I'll stop them!

Jesse: If they're no coal mines, where will the men work? How will they feed their families? They can't live off the land because the soil is too poor and there's not enough good farm land in the whole county. What do you want them to do, make moonshine?

Ollie: Better than coal mining. Besides, I heard you did your share of making and selling. I heard you drank enough moonshine to float a raft down the Big Sandy River.

Jesse: I've done a lot of things I'm not proud of.

Ollie: Is running off and leaving Mom one of them? You think I don't know you were engaged to my mother? Dad sure knows!

Jesse makes a sudden move and Ollie raises his pistol.

Ollie: Preacher, I'll shoot you if I have to. I shot that company jeep at least 125 yards away. Shot two tires and when they tried to backtrack, I got the other two. They're not hurt bad, except maybe their pride. The Jeep ended up in a ditch. I could've killed them but I didn't.

Jesse: Ollie, I know you're not a killer. I know you feel betrayed, but there's a right way to resolve this. Listen to me Ollie. You still got land! I've made a will and my land and house belongs to you and your mom.

Ollie: You're lying or crazy. Probably both.

Jesse: Have I ever told you a lie?

Ollie: None that I've caught you in. But why would you give Mom and me your land? It don't make sense. But wait a minute. You still love my mother, don't you? That's it! You're still in love with her.

Jesse: It's eight of the prettiest acres around. Remember that time you hunted pheasant on my property. You said it was the most wild turkey, grouse and pheasant you'd ever seen. It's all yours, if you'll put down that gun.

Ollie: Preacher, you best be quiet now. There's no way I can make you understand. A couple of years ago, you preached a sermon on the twenty-third psalm. I don't put much stock in preaching, but what you said that day stuck. That psalm talked about lying down in green pastures beside still waters. You said God commands us to love and care for the land. Well, that's what I'm doing. Have you ever loved something so much it don't make sense? You don't have any idea what I'm talking about, do you?

Jesse: Ollie, help me to understand.

Ollie: I'm wasting my breath, but here goes. Years ago, about two dozen families owned big tracts of land. They claimed their people got the land after the Civil War ended. Some folks even brag they could trace their land back to Daniel Boone's days. They're lying, but it don't matter because it's all gone now. I know of only two families that own at least 25 acres.

Jesse: Things change Ollie.

Ollie: And it's not always for the best. Use to, when families had a reunion, 100 people might show up. Family meant something then. But when they broke up the land, things started to change. The kids inherited a few acres here and there but they stopped farming. Hardly anybody even plants a garden now. After a few years, the kids sold off the land and moved away or into the mining camp and started buying everything from the company store.

Jesse: Ollie, I agree with you. But what's done is done. You can't unscramble an egg.

Ollie: No, but you can try. When you own land you're free. When people own the land, they care about each other. But when people lose the land, they lose something and they can't get it back. When time passes, people forget it ever existed. When people grow their own food, it changes the way they look at life. Use to, people loaded their pickups with stuff they raised and went into the camp and sold it dirt cheap. It was a way to be part of something.

Jesse: Ollie, you can pass the land down to your children.

Ollie: I remember when we use to have company before Dad got so ornery. Before they'd leave, Mom would have me pick them a mess of beans, a dozen ears of corn, tomatoes or whatever else was in the garden. Now, the same people meet at the company store and they hardly speak. They can't look each other in the eye. It's like they're ashamed of what they let happen.

Jesse: You can raise anything on my land. It belongs to you and your mom, lock, stock and barrel.

Ollie: You're crazy as I am. It wouldn't be the same. When land's been in a family for generations, there's a spirit that lives on it. Oh, I don't mean like a ghost or something silly like that. But it speaks to you. Say you have 100 acres, if you sell it off a little at a time, you cut a piece of the heart out. Finally, the land dies and things stop growing. That's why the soil is so poor now. Is this making sense to you?

Jesse: Ollie, you and I are more alike than you know.

Ollie: I remember when I was 12, I found a fifth of scotch hidden in Dad's closet. He saved it for a special occasion, but I couldn't resist tasting it. Every time I took a sip, I'd fill it back up with water. After a year, it was nothing but colored water. When Dad finally took a drink, he about gagged. He laid the switch to me for that. Now it's the same way with the land. It's been diluted so much there's nothing left. It has no heart, no spirit, no soul. You think I'm crazy don't you? I'm through talking. It's time for action.

Ollie looks through his field glasses, chuckles and hands them to Jesse who spots Moberly and Whitaker limping in the distance.

Ollie: Lord, that's funny. One is limping with his right leg and the other with his left. If you put the two of them together, you might make a halfway decent man, but I doubt it.

When Ollie takes another peek through the field glasses, Jesse grabs at the pistol. Ollie fires a shot grazing Jesse's shoulder. Ollie then lights the fuse.

Ollie: Preacher, I'll put a bullet between your eyes if I have to. Now, let's get up that hill behind those rocks. I hope your shoulder ain't hurt too bad. Mom would skin me alive for hurting you. Don't worry, I won't tell Dad nothing we talked about. But a blind man could see how you care for Mom. Get down now. She's ready to blow. When I looked through my binoculars, the fools was limping fast so they'll be here before long.

The explosion rips a twelve-foot wide hole in the earthen dam and water pours through the opening, roaring down the narrow valley, felling small trees and tumbling boulders like marbles. However, the dam holds.

Ollie: I can't believe it. I used enough dynamite to blow the whole thing down. What went wrong?

Jesse: Ollie, It takes a lot of dynamite. It's not like the movies.

Ollie: Guess I'll have to do it again.

Ollie and Jessie are caught off guard when the entire center of the damn collapses and a river roars down the hollow in the direction of the church. It's as if a giant hand reaches down and lifts the small church off the ground. But as quickly as the water rises it begins to recede, gently setting the church house on a level stretch of land atop a hill.

Jesse: The church didn't break apart. It's a miracle.

Ollie: Preacher man, looks like I used enough dynamite after all.

Jesse: I can't believe it. The water set the church house down where it should've been built in the first place. I hope the structure is still sound.

Ollie: Pastor, it's like you say-the good Lord works in mysterious ways. I hope your church ain't damaged too bad.

Jesse: Ollie, I see them coming. You better get out of here.

Still hiding behind the rocks, Ollie raises his rifle to fire but Jesse jerks it away and tosses it on the ground. Ollie stands and lunges for the gun but Jesse, despite his wounded shoulder, strikes Ollie with a right, left and right again. Jesse catches a wobbly Ollie and eases him to the ground. Jesse then searches Ollie's pockets and finds some blasting caps, lighter, a short piece of fuse and a pocketknife. Within minutes, Moberly and Whitaker struggle up the hill pointing a rifle and shotgun at Jesse.

Moberly: I can't believe it! You fools! Why? Why? It's just senseless destruction! Are you people so stupid you can't see we're trying to do something good here? My God, such senseless destruction! If you people had your way, we'd be back in the stone age. Handcuff Collins and check on that idiot lying on the ground. Collins, what in God's name is wrong with you?

Jesse: I guess I was having a bad day.

Whitaker: I'll show you a bad day.

Whitaker slaps Jesse repeatedly, but then spits in his face. Jesse flinches and strains to free his hands that are cuffed behind his back.

Moberly: Whitaker, that's enough of that. Control yourself. He's trying to provoke you. See if Ollie can stand up. Did a rock from the blast strike him?

Whitaker: The blast should've blown his head off.

Moberly: Alright Jesse, let's hear it. Why did you and Poser do it?

Jesse: I quit smoking recently and I guess it's made me a bit cranky.

Whitaker balls up his fist to strike Collins, but a harsh glance from Moberly changes his mind.

Moberly: Tell me what happened? Make a clean break and it might go a little easier for you. Just tell me why you did it? Was it a personal vendetta against the coal company? Go ahead and get it off your chest.

Jesse: Alright. Ollie caught me lighting the fuse and tried to stop me. We fought. You can see the results.

Moberly: Why? Why would you do such a thing?

Jesse: I didn't want a dam at the mouth of the hollow above my church, so I blew it up. Search my pockets and you'll find a couple of blasting caps.

Moberly: You trying to tell me Poser had nothing to do with this? Why should I believe you?

Jesse: Because it's the truth. I was going to frame him, but I changed my mind. I knew he was upset with his dad when he ran off into the woods. I figured you would blame him for what happened.

Moberly: What else happened? Tell us what you did?

Jesse: I did some other damage. You know what it was.

Whitaker: You tell us wise guy.

Jesse: If I told you Whitaker, you'd just forget. You don't look real bright to me. You're so slow I can't even get mad at you.

Whitaker: I'm warning you smart mouth.

Moberly: That's enough Burke. Can't you see he's baiting you?

Jesse: Whitaker, I heard you quit sixth grade because you hated recess. Is that right? What's the company paying you? I bet you make half of what a miner earns.

Whitaker: Keep it up wise guy. Nothing I'd like better than to bust a hillbilly's hard head.

Jesse: Whitaker, you'll never make it to retirement. They'll fire you a month before you get enough time in. You'll end up begging for a job working underground. You'll spend the rest of your life using a coal shovel because you're too dumb and lazy to operate mining equipment safely.

Whitaker becomes enraged and strikes Jesse with his fist. Jesse shakes off the blow and rams his good shoulder into Whitaker's stomach knocking him back against a rock causing him to strike his head. Jesse runs surprisingly fast for someone with his hands cuffed behind his back. A furious Moberly stops in his tracks.

Moberly: Collins, you're a poor excuse for a preacher! Blake, we'll catch Collins and take him to the police station when the other guards get here! I'm tired of this foolishness! We'll take them in separately. I want these hoodlums put in separate rooms to interrogate them. Now get that idiot Poser to his feet.

Whitaker struggles to stand, grabs Ollie's rifle and fires two shots into Jesse's back. Jesse falls quickly. Moberly turns and jerks the rifle away from a still woozy Whitaker who has blood flowing down his face. Whitaker stumbles backward, plops on the ground and holds his head.

Moberly: You fool! You miserable fool! What's wrong with you? Are you insane? Am I the only sane person on this mountain? Whitaker, couldn't you see he was lying! He was covering up for Poser. Do you want a guilty man to go free? Get out of my sight! You make me sick to my stomach! You just resigned whether you know it or not. But don't leave town. You have a lot to explain to the police. (Lights fade)

Scene Five

Lights rise in the cabin as the Poser family sits at the kitchen table. No one eats despite a tableful of food. Tension hovers in the air. Will looks out the window, Hankins reads his Bible, Ollie lays his head on the table and Thalia stares at her coffee cup.

Although Jesse died the day before, somehow a part of him lingers. A spirit begins to move about the room, touching, challenging and consoling. Silence eventually yields as Will resumes the discussion.

Will: Why should we bury Jesse in the family cemetery? He's not family, even though some of you act like he is.

Thalia: Because the church won't bury him in their cemetery.

Will: What's wrong with the town cemetery? It's not like Jesse will know.

Thalia: Jesse should be buried here.

Will: I say no.

Thalia: Say what you want, but he'll be buried here.

Will: You think I don't know? Do you think I'm blind? How naïve am I suppose to be?

Thalia: You don't know anything. Jesse was good. Do you understand? Just plain good.

Will: Yeah, he was so good his church members turned their backs on him. I for one can't blame them. And you, making a scene like you did! I'm ashamed to show my face in public now. I can't go to that church ever again.

Thalia: They won't survive without the ten dollars you give every year.

Will: This is no time to be sarcastic. Anyway, what I give is between me and my conscience. But I bet they wouldn't take a $1,000 from us after what you did to Deacon Cartwright. If you'd just slapped him it wouldn't be so bad. For God's sake Thalia, you throw a punch like a prizefighter. You a woman and fighting like a man!

Thalia: Is it any worse than a man fighting like a woman?

Will: You always have to play with words. All Deacon Cartwright said was Jesse wasn't who he pretended to be, and the church was better off without him.

Thalia: Jesse was who he said he was and that terrified the deacons. If Jesus walked in that church, Deacon Cartwright would be the first one to kick him. Some people look for heaven so high up and so far away, they can't tolerate a little bit of heaven on earth.

Hankins: If you want to punch somebody, Hawthorne is a good pick. Half the church has hit him and the other half is thinking about it.

Will: Dad, stay out of this.

Ollie: Last week, the people loved Jesse. Now they've turned against him. How can people love you one minute and hate you the next? They don't know he took my place. Why would he do that? He never done anything wrong, but he was punished for what I done.

Hankins: I agree with Thalia. Jesse should be buried up there on the hill.

Will: This is none of your concern.

Hankins: I'm making it my business. Like the Good Book says Will, you're forever learning, but never understanding.

Will: Who are you to quote the Bible to me?

Hankins: You always say how things need to change in the mountains. Well, a change has come over this house. Your bullying days are over.

Will: How dare you talk to me that way?

Hankins: I can't hold my tongue any longer. Will, you're an ignorant man. The more you know the less you understand.

Ollie: God, I feel like he's still here. He's in this room. Jesse is here and he wants to tell us something.

Will: Good grief, boy. Don't start falling apart on me now.

Ollie: I've got to get it off my chest. I'm thinking about confessing to the police. I've got to confess!

Will: Don't be a dang fool. What good would come of it? Nobody knows the truth but us. It's going to stay that way.

Thalia: I don't know how I feel. Part of me wants Ollie to confess. But a part of me feels if we bury Jesse here, we can move on. It's a way of honoring him. It's a way of making amends. I'm sorry Will, but if you can't appreciate what Jesse has done for this family, then you're a fool.

Will: Don't talk to me like that. I've never hit you in my life but…

Hankins: And you ain't going to now. You touch a hair on Thalia's head and the three of us will beat you to a pulp.

Will: Ollie, are you going let him talk to your dad that way?

Ollie: I love you Dad, but I haven't liked you in years.

Will: The whole family is against me. You've all turned against me. Well, I'm still opposed to doing it. What would people think?

Thalia: Why should it matter? Our son is free because of Jesse.

Ollie: I should go right now and confess. Why did he do it? Why did he take my place?

Will's hard exterior is starting to crack. But Will is terrified that any hint of kindness might be misconstrued as weakness.

Will: Because, because, he, he, he loved your mother! He loved your mother! He's never stopped loving her!

Thalia: Yes Will, Jesse loved me but not in the way you think. Jesse looked past people's meanness and flaws and saw them the way heaven sees them-weak, scared, foolish, but still worth loving. We're all worth loving. Even you, Will.

Will: You don't know. You just don't know.

Thalia: You're right Will. I don't know. And I don't know you at all. Frankly, I don't want to know you.

Will: If you only knew.

Hankins: Jesse will be buried on the hill and that's final. And there's something else we should do. We can make amends by repairing the church. The foundation was weakened pretty bad.

Will: Dad, I said stay out of this.

Hankins: Son, you've got so much anger and bitterness in you. You're so twisted inside, you can't tell good from bad.

Ollie: Granddad, what are you talking about?

Will: Dad, don't say another word!

Hankins: Remember how close Will and I were when he was young? I taught him to throw a football, hunt, fish. Together we rebuilt an engine for my old work truck. No father and son could have been closer. But it ended. It's all different now.

Will: Dad, I'm warning you! Don't say another word!

Ollie: What happened to change things? Tell me?

Will: Don't do it Dad. I'm warning you! Once you let the hounds out of the pen, it's not easy to get them back in.

Hankins: I never thought I'd see this day, but it's here. It's been long overdue.

Ollie: What are you guys talking about?

Thalia: Will, this family's survival is at stake. This is your last chance with me. If you have anything worth saying, you better speak up.

Will: Alright! Alright! You want to know the truth. I'll tell you the truth!

Thalia: Go ahead and say it.

Will: You think you want to hear this but you don't.

Thalia: You've had your chance. It's over.

When Thalia stands to leave Will leaps from his chair so fast it overturns.

Will: Please sit down. Sit down and listen. I've wanted to get this off my chest for a long time. I've wanted somebody to hurt like I've been hurting. This family has been living a lie. Hankins Poser is an imposter. He's not my father!

Thalia: Good Lord, Will. What are you saying?

Ollie: It's a lie! You lied about not selling the land! You lie about everything!

Hankins: It's true. Now tell everything Will.

Will: I've said enough. I'll say no more.

Hankins: You haven't said anything. Tell them or I will.

Will: You remember when I quit high school my junior year? One month of school left and I just walked away.

I had an A, three B's and a C. If I'd studied more I could've made all A's.

Ollie: Why did you quit?

Will: One day I had to get a copy of my birth certificate for something at school. I don't even remember what for. Mom and Dad, I mean Mom and Hankins were out shopping. I was looking through an old trunk in the closet and found a bunch of papers and discovered Hankins Poser was not my father. I've lived with this lie for years. I've lost all feeling for my so-called mother and father. They're nothing but liars, hypocrites and phonies.

Hankins: Shut your mouth! Don't you dare tarnish the name of your mother. There was never a wife or mother as good as my Sarah. She was your mother. I was and am your dad.

Will: My father was some man in Cincinnati. Don't know who he is. Don't care to know. I don't have a father.

Hankins: Anybody can be a birth father. To be a dad you have to love and care for your own. I remember when you were little, I couldn't wait to get home from the mines and put you on my knee and sing to you. When I had a bad day at work, I'd think about something you said and it would cheer me up. It would make my day.

I remember when you were in first grade and we bought you a Roy Rogers lunch box. I came home from work one day and you'd taken a red crayon and marked all over a wall. You wore it down to a nub. I made you sit on the couch for an hour and wouldn't let you listen to Superman on the radio.

When we got ready to eat supper a little after five, there was a knock on the door. A neighbor saw you walking down the street by yourself. You told him you were running away from home. You'd packed your Roy Rogers lunch box plumb full of candy bars, snack cakes and a can of beer. Sarah and me laughed about that for a week.

Ollie: Dad, you saved that lunch box all these years. You gave it to me when I was in first grade. I still have it. One day I plan to give it to my son.

Hankins: Will, I have so many wonderful memories of your mother, brothers and you. Precious memories.

Will: How could you forgive her?

Hankins: How could I not forgive her? How do you judge somebody's entire life by one mistake? The Good Lord knows I've made plenty myself. I made a mistake by not telling you. Why can't you forgive me? What kind of world do we make when nobody forgives nobody? When we do that we're playing God. Son, I love you, but I don't know what to say or do to reach you. I don't know. I just don't know.

Silence engulfs the cabin. It has been a cold, damp, overcast day. Although it is only three in the afternoon, it feels like five o'clock. The sun, intimidated most of the day, begins to flex its muscles and peeps from behind the clouds. Suddenly, it becomes a bright ball of light. Shadows begin to run along the wall and disappear into the ceiling.

Will holds his head in his hands and begins to sob. It has been years since he has showed any real emotion. The four sense something has changed. A burden lifts as Ollie and Hankins stand and put their arms around Will. Thalia is crying, but the pain has left her face. She seems at peace.

Now there is a spirit of healing in the air. The shadows are gone, perhaps never to return. Something flashes past outside the kitchen window and everyone turns to look. Finally, Ollie begins to talk.

Ollie: We'll can get our tools and go to the church and help. There's a few guys over there working now.

Thalia: I'll pack a picnic basket. We've got enough food here to feed half the church. There's a couple of hours of daylight left. You boys can work until you give out.

Hankins: Don't take much for me to give out. I can't play a game of checkers anymore without getting winded.

Ollie: Don't worry Granddad, you can smoke your pipe, read your Bible and give orders. You can be the boss.

Will: Thalia, I, I, uh…

Thalia: I know Will, I know.

Will: Where do I begin…

Thalia: At the beginning Will. At the beginning. (Lights fade)

Epilogue

Lights rise six months later at Jesse's gravesite. Thalia stands before Jesse's grave with head bowed. It is early May, and a boisterous mass of wildflowers cling to the steep slopes of Harlan County. Along all the mountain ridges, flowers stand proudly and wave at passersby. It's as if nature is celebrating. Poser land now belongs to the company except for the family cemetery and a few acres. Less than 200 yards away, an access road sneaks up the hillside to one of the company's mine sites.

Thalia picks an armful of wildflowers to place on Jesse's grave. She kneels, prays, and then stands with difficulty. Her right knee is getting worse. A sweet wind caresses her face. Somehow, Jesse's presence is as real in death as in life.

Also, Thalia's appearance has changed. She is less a tomboy and more feminine. Recently, she cut her long hair, gained a few pounds and bought new, bright-colored clothes. There is still a wisp of sadness about her, laced with peace and contentment. She is almost happy.

Thalia: Jesse, I hope you like my new outfit.

Jesse: Thalia, you grow more beautiful every day.

Thalia: Why didn't you tell me before?

Jesse: I did, just not in words. But I knew you knew.

Thalia: I could always feel your love, but I just needed you to say it. I remember that time when you were sick in bed for three days and somehow I knew it. I woke up at four o'clock that first morning and felt a crazy need to fix chicken soup. Ollie had a fever and I repeatedly put a cold cloth to his forehead. That last day, when his fever broke, I stopped worrying about you. When Ollie got better, I knew you were well. I don't know why, but I knew it.

Jesse: You were there.

Thalia: Jesse, if you're gone how can you be here? There's so much I don't understand.

Jesse: I'm still learning myself, but we aren't meant to understand everything. There are mysteries in death as well as life.

Thalia: One minute I'm happy, the next I'm sad. How can that be? Is something wrong with me?

Jesse: You're on the verge of an important discovery-that chains are made of paper and can be broken.

Thalia: But why didn't I break them before?

Jesse: Because someone told you chains were made of iron and you believed the lie.

Thalia: Jesse, how can I feel your love so strongly?

Jesse: There are no barriers to love other than what we erect. Love doesn't end at death, it just seeks new paths. Love is a mist, a vapor that can penetrate the heavens and return to earth. Once love exists, it can't be destroyed. It can be denied, ignored, or disguised, but it's unrelenting. It doesn't give up. It never ends.

Thalia: I've got good news to tell you. Ollie is spending the next six months fixing up your house. I mean his house. Then he's going to college. He wants to become an architect and return to Harlan County to build houses.

Jesse: I'm so proud of him.

Thalia: Now you won't believe this. Clive McAlister and the company strip-mined a bunch of hills and filled in hollows with the rock and dirt. They created flat land where there was none. The people made them keep their promise to build houses for the miners. Now they're going to donate 40 acres to build a whole neighborhood. Guess what they're going to name it? It'll be a section of town named Collins.

Jesse: I can see the last house being built. It's a nice community.

Thalia: Will and I are attending a church in town. I'm singing in the choir. Will is even going to church on Wednesday night. Hard to believe, isn't it?

Jesse: Not from where I dwell.

Thalia: Did you know we're going to marriage counseling? We have to go all the way to Lexington.

Jesse: I'm the one who told you to go.

Thalia: Can I learn to love him again?

Jesse: I told you Thalia, love changes shape, but it never dies. It returns in the way it's needed most. But if you can't forgive, you can't love. If you can't love, you can't feel. If you can't feel, you'll sleepwalk until it's too late. It's up to you and Will.

Thalia: Why did you have to leave? Wasn't there some other way?

Jesse: Thalia, I'm still in the dark about a lot of things.

Thalia: Jesse, I can't come back again.

Jesse: I know.

Thalia: Goodbye, Jesse.

Jesse: Goodbye, Thalia.

As Thalia leaves the cemetery, she begins to hum softly. She passes a tree and hears birds singing. Suddenly she bursts forth in song:

> *Whenever I hear the church bells ring*
> *My spirit soars and I joyfully sing*
> *And breathe a little heaven on earth*
> *Just to know what I'm truly worth*

Suddenly, birds begin to sing from every tree on the hillside. Thalia throws back her head and laughs as the singing escorts her down the hill and safely on her way.

The End